READ & LISTEN OS MELHORES CONTOS DO SÉCULO XX EM VERSÃO ORIGINAL NA ÍNTEGRA

*"Sometimes all we need
is a fine, short story."*

Martins Fontes

Toni Morrison
Recitatif

•

Doris Lessing
To Room Nineteen

© 1983 por Confirmation: An Anthology of African American Women. Editado por Amiri (LeRoi Jones) e Amina Baraka. William Morrow and Co., Ltd., NY.
© 1968 por Doris Lessing. Reimpressão com permissão de Jonathan Clowes Ltd., London, em nome de Doris Lessing.
© 2011 Martins Editora Livraria Ltda., São Paulo, para a presente edição.

Publisher	*Evandro Mendonça Martins Fontes*
Coordenação editorial	*Anna Dantes*
Produção editorial	*Alyne Azuma*
Tradução	*Betty Nisembaum*
Revisão	*Denise Roberti Camargo*
	André Albert
	Dinarte Zorzanelli da Silva
Biografias e apresentações	*Laura Fernández*
Locução de "Recitatif"	*Amber Ockrassa*
Locução de "To Room Nineteen"	*Ayesha Mendham*
Gravação	*RecLab*
Técnico	*Francesc Gosalves*

Dados Internacionais de Catalogação na Publicação (CIP)
(Câmara Brasileira do Livro, SP, Brasil)

Morrison, Toni, 1931-.
 Recitatif / Toni Morrison. To room nineteen / Doris Lessing / [tradução Betty Nisembaum]. – 1. ed. – São Paulo : Martins Martins Fontes, 2011.

 Título original: Recitatif ; To room nineteen.
 Inclui CD.
 ISBN 978-85-8063-010-7

 1. Contos ingleses 2. Contos norte-americanos I. Lessing, Doris, 1919-. II. Título. III. Título: To room nineteen.

11-02232   CDD-823.91
                                                                                                                          -813

Índices para catálogo sistemático:
1. Contos : Literatura inglesa 823.91
2. Contos : Literatura norte-americana 813

Todos os direitos desta edição para o Brasil reservados à
Martins Editora Livraria Ltda.
Av. Dr. Arnaldo, 2076
01255-000 São Paulo SP Brasil
Tel. (11) 3116.0000
info@martinseditora.com.br
www.martinsmartinsfontes.com.br

SUMÁRIO

INTRODUÇÃO... 9

Toni Morrison
BIOGRAFIA.. 13
APRESENTAÇÃO DO CONTO 15
Recitatif... 17

Doris Lessing
BIOGRAFIA.. 53
APRESENTAÇÃO DO CONTO 55
To Room Nineteen... 57

INTRODUÇÃO
Dê um passo além e leia os clássicos em versão original

Para muitos de nós, ler em versão original supõe um desafio por vezes irrealizável. Habituados a nossa própria língua, ficamos frustrados quando não entendemos todas as palavras de um texto. Quantas vezes deixamos um livro de lado porque não queremos consultar o dicionário a toda hora? Essa consulta (quase sempre obrigatória) se soma ao desconhecimento das referências culturais, à dificuldade de perceber os matizes, a ironia do autor etc. Logo nos aborrecemos por não conseguir compreender a essência do relato e acabamos fechando o livro e buscando a versão traduzida.

Na coleção READ & LISTEN a leitura e audição do texto original produzem experiências tão únicas quanto a de contemplar uma pintura em vez de sua reprodução. Não só se aprende como também se desfruta e assimila o verdadeiro espírito do relato.

Aqui, os leitores podem ter acesso aos melhores contos dos mais respeitados autores de língua inglesa, com as ferramentas necessárias para compreender os textos em sua totalidade.

Foi-se o tempo de ler com o dicionário do lado. Cada conto inclui um extenso glossário para que não seja necessário interromper a leitura. Além de todas as palavras que você pode não entender, ele apresenta referências culturais, deixa claras as nuances e permite compreender todos os toques irônicos de cada conto. Para quem quer praticar a compreensão oral ou simplesmente ouvir o texto enquanto o lê, nada mais simples. Ponha o CD com a versão em áudio dos contos para tocar, sente-se, relaxe e deixe que um locutor nativo conte a história. Porque não há maneira melhor de colocar ao seu alcance essas obras-primas do que rompendo as barreiras que o mantiveram longe delas durante tanto tempo.

Quem tem medo dos clássicos?

E por falar em clássicos... Nossa seleção se guiou por várias premissas: em primeiro lugar, os contos tinham de ser sugestivos e não muito complexos; em segundo lugar, tinham de representar o mundo próprio de cada autor. Clássicos em miniatura, inesquecíveis, os contos desta coleção devem ser lidos com cuidado, degustando cada frase, cada palavra. São obras capazes de transformar seus personagens em alguém conhecido, quase familiar, que poderia ser seu melhor amigo.

Acreditamos que, depois de tanto tempo aprendendo inglês, chegou seu momento de desfrutar. Você merece.

Toni Morrison
Recitatif

"Suddenly, in just a pulse beat, twenty years disappeared and all of it came rushing back."

BIOGRAFIA
Toni Morrison

Quando criança, foi muito pobre. Nasceu em Lorain, um povoado no estado do Ohio, em 1931. Chamaram-na Chloe Anthony, daí o Toni (diminutivo carinhoso como a família se referia a ela). O sobrenome do seu pai era Wofford, mas Toni trocou para Morrison quando se casou com Harold, o primeiro rapaz que a conquistou. O casamento durou seis anos (de 1958 a 1964). Quando se separaram, Morrison começou a escrever. Seu primeiro romance ficou pronto em 1970, ano em que foi publicado. Intitulou-o *O olho mais azul*. Faltavam 23 anos para que lhe fosse concedido o Nobel de Literatura por uma intensa carreira literária centrada nos problemas raciais que afligiam seu país (e o resto do planeta) desde tempos longínquos.

Antes de se casar com Harold e de descobrir sua vocação para a literatura, Toni mudou-se para Washington a fim de estudar na Universidade de Howard. Dali se transferiu para Cornell, onde concluiu o mestrado em Filologia Inglesa, em 1955. Logo se tornou professora. Deu aulas de inglês na Universidade do Texas até 1964, ano em que deixou tudo para virar editora da divisão norte-americana da Random House. Nessa época morava em Nova York com seus dois filhos e dava aulas esporádicas na Universidade Estadual de Nova York, em Albany. Ainda era professora ali quando publicou seu primeiro livro.

Naquela época, Morrison tinha quase 40 anos. A protagonista do romance é uma menina que sonha ter os olhos da mesma cor que os das bonecas de suas amigas de classe (brancas). Três anos depois, Morrison publicou *Sula*, e, em 1977, *Song of Salo-*

mon [A canção de Salomão], uma espécie de livro romântico de grande alcance que lhe rendeu o Prêmio da Crítica (National Book Critics Awards). De qualquer maneira, Toni Morrison só se tornaria um clássico uma década depois, quando publicou *Amada* (1987), a história de uma escrava que decide acabar com a vida de sua filha para livrá-la da escravidão. *Amada* ganhou o Pulitzer em 1987 e levou a autora às portas do Nobel de Literatura, finalmente concedido a ela em 1993, quando tinha publicado apenas seis romances.

A luta pela liberdade, os direitos civis, o amor, a amizade e, acima de tudo, a convivência racial são alguns dos temas que a narrativa de Morrison, primeira escritora negra a ganhar o Nobel, explora. Após a concessão do prêmio, publicou outros três romances; o último, *Compaixão*, conta a história de uma jovem afro-americana do século XVII (volta à época da escravidão, do racismo, da segregação) e é também uma história de amor e de amizade.

Toni Morrison, que foi professora de Humanidades na Universidade de Princeton até 2006 e é membro da Academia Americana de Artes e Letras, só escreveu um conto em todos estes anos. "Recitatif" é a comovente história de duas amigas (uma branca e outra negra) separadas após uma infância em comum que se reencontram ao longo da vida de forma fortuita e se sentem perseguidas pelos fantasmas do passado.

APRESENTAÇÃO DO CONTO
Recitatif

A mãe de Twyla dança nos horários menos oportunos. A de Roberta sempre está doente. Ou assim dizem. A única coisa que esta faz é ir de um lado para o outro com uma Bíblia enorme. As meninas compartilham um quarto em St. Bonny's, um orfanato. Elas são as únicas que recebem visitas de suas mães (as das demais estão no céu). Uma menina branca e outra negra unidas frente ao inimigo: as meninas que pintam os lábios (as maiores). Há também uma estranha ajudante de cozinha, muda, da qual todo mundo ri. Mas Twyla ria dela? E era negra?

As meninas abandonam o orfanato e se reencontram ao menos cinco vezes no tempo. A primeira vez que se reveem, após todos aqueles anos compartilhando um quarto, é maluca demais. Roberta, acompanhada de duas crianças, vai ao encontro de Jimi Hendrix (é o que ela disse) e finge não conhecer Twyla.

Mas o que acontece nos outros reencontros? E por que o fantasma de Maggie, a mulher muda e estranha, se faz presente em todos eles? O que aconteceu realmente no orfanato?

"Recitatif" é o único conto que Toni Morrison escreveu. Foi publicado em 1983 e comentado pela própria Morrison no volume *Playing in the Dark: Whiteness and the Literary Imagination*. A escritora o chamou de "experimento" sobre duas meninas que ficaram marcadas por um acontecimento relacionado com um conflito racial. O título do conto faz referência ao interlúdio de uma ópera. De fato, os encontros sucessivos das protagonistas ao longo da vida (um total de cinco) são em parte interlúdios da ação, pequenos momentos à parte nos quais as protagonistas dão pinceladas de um passado que não deixou de atormentá-las de tempos em tempos. Desde Jimi Hendrix até uma xícara de café uns dias antes do Natal, o terno e ao mesmo tempo arrepiante conto de Morrison é uma espécie de registro de uma amizade que se manteve intacta (como a porcelana de um vaso que nunca se toca) ao longo de toda uma vida.

Evidentemente, "Recitatif" é um fiel retrato da produção novelística de sua autora. É um experimento, como ela mesma afirmou, porém sobre um material familiar: o racismo, aquele de meados do século, em choque com o pensamento contemporâneo e encarnado em duas meninas, uma delas negra. Racismo estendido à marginalização nua e crua, já que a personagem atacada pelas duas meninas e as mais velhas que pintam os lábios é, na realidade, uma senhora mais velha e muda. No entanto, o conto trata também da amizade, tema absolutamente recorrente em toda a narrativa de Morrison.

Assim, ler esta autora em versão original parece-nos um luxo do qual não podíamos prescindir. O glossário incluído em cada página desta edição evitará a sempre cansativa visita ao dicionário e permitirá a você saborear um conto que é um mundo em si mesmo. Um mundo que contém outros mundos e um pedaço substancial da obra de sua autora. Para aqueles que se atreverem a dar um passo a mais, ouvir o áudio do conto não só colocará à prova a sua compreensão oral, como também os transportará a outro universo, no qual a crueldade adolescente se une ao universo adulto desprovido de piedade.

LAURA FERNÁNDEZ

Recitatif

My mother danced all night and Roberta's was sick¹. That's why we were taken to St. Bonny's. People want to put their arms around you when you tell them you were in a shelter², but it really wasn't bad. No big long room with one hundred beds like Bellevue³. There were four to a room, and when Roberta and me came, there was a shortage⁴ of state kids⁵, so we were the only ones assigned to 406 and could go from bed to bed if we wanted to. And we wanted to, too. We changed beds every night and for the whole four months we were there we never picked one out⁶ as our own permanent bed.

It didn't start out that way. The minute I walked in and the Big Bozo⁷ introduced us, I got sick to my stomach. It was one thing to be taken out of your own bed early in the morning—it was something else to be stuck⁸ in a strange place with a girl from a whole other race. And Mary, that's my mother, she was right⁹. Every now and then¹⁰ she would stop dancing long enough to tell me something important and one of the things she said was that they never washed their hair and they smelled funny¹¹. Roberta sure did. Smell funny, I mean. So when the Big Bozo (nobody ever called her Mrs. Itkin, just like nobody

---

1 **sick:** doente • 2 **shelter:** abrigo • 3 **Bellevue:** nome de um abrigo • 4 **shortage:** escassez • 5 **state kids:** crianças sob a tutela do Estado • 6 **picked one out:** escolhemos uma • 7 **Big Bozo:** apelido da sra. Itkin • 8 **to be stuck:** estar presa • 9 **she was right:** tinha razão • 10 **every now and then:** de vez em quando • 11 **they smelled funny:** tinham um cheiro esquisito

ever said St. Bonaventure)—when she said, "Twyla, this is Roberta. Roberta, this is Twyla. Make each other welcome[1]." I said, "My mother won't like you putting me in here."

"Good," said Bozo. "Maybe then she'll come and take you home."

How's that for mean[2]? If Roberta had laughed I would have killed her, but she didn't. She just walked over to the window[3] and stood with her back to us[4].

"Turn around[5]," said the Bozo. "Don't be rude[6]. Now Twyla. Roberta. When you hear a loud buzzer[7], that's the call for dinner. Come down to the first floor. Any fights and no movie[8]." And then, just to make sure we knew what we would be missing[9], "The Wizard of Oz"[10].

Roberta must have thought I meant that my mother would be mad about[11] my being put in the shelter. Not about rooming[12] with her, because as soon as Bozo left she came over to me and said, "Is your mother sick too?"

"No," I said. "She just likes to dance all night."

"Oh," she nodded her head[13] and I liked the way she understood things so fast. So for the moment it didn't matter that we looked like salt and pepper[14] standing there and that's what the other kids called us sometimes. We were eight years old and got F's[15] all the time. Me because I couldn't remember what I read

---

1 **make each other welcome:** tratem-se bem • 2 **how's that for mean?:** que maldade! • 3 **walked over to the window:** se aproximou da janela • 4 **with her back to us:** de costas para nós • 5 **turn around:** vire-se • 6 **rude:** mal-educada • 7 **buzzer:** campainha • 8 **any fights and no movie:** se brigarem, não vai ter filme • 9 **what we would be missing:** o que estaríamos perdendo • 10 **The Wizard of Oz:** O mágico de Oz • 11 **would be mad about:** ficaria brava por • 12 **rooming:** dividir o quarto com • 13 **she nodded her head:** assentiu com a cabeça • 14 **like salt and pepper:** como sal e pimenta (referência às raças das duas meninas, branca e negra) • 15 **F's:** nota vermelha

or what the teacher said. And Roberta because she couldn't read at all and didn't even listen to the teacher. She wasn't good at anything except jacks[1], at which she was a killer[2]: pow scoop pow scoop pow scoop.

We didn't like each other all that much at first, but nobody else wanted to play with us because we weren't real orphans with beautiful dead parents in the sky. We were dumped[3]. Even the New York City Puerto Ricans and the upstate[4] Indians ignored us. All kinds of kids were in there, black ones, white ones, even two Koreans. The food was good, though. At least I thought so. Roberta hated it and left whole pieces of things on her plate: Spam[5], Salisbury steak[6]—even jello[7] with fruit cocktail[8] in it, and she didn't care if I ate what she wouldn't. Mary's idea of supper was popcorn and a can of Yoo-Hoo[9]. Hot mashed potatoes[10] and two weenies[11] was like Thanksgiving[12] for me.

It really wasn't bad, St. Bonny's. The big girls on the second floor pushed us around[13] now and then. But that was all. They wore lipstick and eyebrow pencil[14] and wobbled[15] their knees while they watched TV. Fifteen, sixteen, even, some of them were. They were put-out girls[16], scared runaways[17] most of them. Poor little girls who fought their uncles off[18] but

---

1 **jacks:** jogo de pedrinhas • 2 **she was a killer:** era ótima • 3 **we were dumped:** nós tínhamos sido abandonadas • 4 **upstate:** do norte do estado • 5 **Spam:** marca de carne enlatada • 6 **Salisbury steak:** bife de carne moída com molho • 7 **jello:** gelatina • 8 **fruit cocktail:** salada de frutas • 9 **Yoo-Hoo:** bebida achocolatada • 10 **mashed potatoes:** purê de batatas • 11 **weenies:** salsichas • 12 **Thanksgiving:** Ação de Graças • 13 **pushed us around:** nos pertubavam • 14 **eyebrow pencil:** lápis de olho • 15 **wobbled:** tremiam • 16 **put-out girls:** garotas expulsas • 17 **runaways:** fugitivas • 18 **who fought their uncles off:** brigavam para se livrar de seus tios

looked tough[1] to us, and mean[2]. God did they look mean. The staff tried to keep them separate from the younger children, but sometimes they caught us watching them in the orchard[3] where they played radios and danced with each other. They'd light out after us[4] and pull our hair[5] or twist our arms[6]. We were scared of them, Roberta and me, but neither of us wanted the other one to know it. So we got a good list of dirty names[7] we could shout back when we ran from them through the orchard. I used to dream a lot and almost always the orchard was there. Two acres, four maybe, of these little apple trees. Hundreds of them. Empty and crooked[8] like beggar women[9] when I first came to St. Bonny's but fat with[10] flowers when I left. I don't know why I dreamt about that orchard so much. Nothing really happened there. Nothing all that important, I mean. Just the big girls dancing and playing the radio. Roberta and me watching. Maggie fell down[11] there once. The kitchen woman with legs like parentheses. And the big girls laughed at her. We should have helped her up[12], I know, but we were scared of those girls with lipstick and eyebrow pencil. Maggie couldn't talk. The kids said she had her tongue cut out, but I think she was just born that way: mute. She was old and sandy-colored and she worked in the kitchen. I don't know if she was nice or not. I just remember her legs like parentheses and how she rocked[13] when she walked. She worked from early in the morning till two o'clock, and if she was late, if she had too

---

1 **tough:** duronas, violentas • 2 **mean:** más • 3 **orchard:** pomar • 4 **they'd light out after us:** nos perseguiam • 5 **pull our hair:** puxavam nosso cabelo • 6 **twist our arms:** torciam nosso braço • 7 **dirty names:** xingamentos • 8 **crooked:** retorcidos • 9 **beggar women:** mendigas • 10 **fat with:** cheias de • 11 **fell down:** caiu • 12 **we should have helped her up:** deveríamos tê-la ajudado a se levantar • 13 **she rocked:** se balançava

much cleaning and didn't get out till two-fifteen or so, she'd cut through[1] the orchard so she wouldn't miss her bus and have to wait another hour. She wore this really stupid little hat—a kid's hat with ear flaps[2]—and she wasn't much taller than we were. A really awful little hat. Even for a mute, it was dumb dressing like a kid[3] and never saying anything at all.

"But what about if somebody tries to kill her?" I used to wonder about that. "Or what if she wants to cry? Can she cry?"

"Sure," Roberta said. "But just tears. No sounds come out."

"She can't scream?"

"Nope[4]. Nothing."

"Can she hear?"

"I guess."

"Let's call her," I said. And we did.

"Dummy[5]! Dummy!" She never turned her head

"Bow legs[6]! Bow legs!" Nothing. She just rocked on[7], the chin straps[8] of her baby-boy hat swaying[9] from side to side. I think we were wrong. I think she could hear and didn't let on. And it shames me[10] even now to think there was somebody in there after all who heard us call her those names and couldn't tell on us[11].

We got along all right[12], Roberta and me. Changed beds every night, got F's in civics[13] and communication skills and gym. The Bozo was disappointed in us, she said. Out of 130 of

---

1 **she'd cut through:** atravessava • 2 **ear flaps:** protetor de orelhas • 3 **even for a mute, it was dumb dressing like a kid:** mesmo sendo muda, era burrice vestir-se como criança ("dumb" é tanto "mudo"como "estúpido") • 4 **nope:** não (coloquial) • 5 **dummy:** muda • 6 **bow legs:** pernas tortas • 7 **she just rocked on:** continuou se balançando • 8 **chin straps:** cordões do chapéu • 9 **swaying:** balançando-se • 10 **it shames me:** me envergonha • 11 **couldn't tell on us:** não podia nos delatar • 12 **we got along all right:** nos dávamos bem • 13 **civics:** educação moral e cívica

us statecases[1], 90 were under twelve. Almost all were real orphans with beautiful dead parents in the sky. We were the only ones dumped and the only ones with F's in three classes including gym. So we got along—what with[2] her leaving whole pieces of things on her plate and being nice about not asking questions.

I think it was the day before Maggie fell down that we found out our mothers were coming to visit us on the same Sunday. We had been at the shelter twenty-eight days (Roberta twenty-eight and a half) and this was their first visit with us. Our mothers would come at ten o'clock in time[3] for chapel, then lunch with us in the teachers' lounge[4]. I thought if my dancing mother met her sick mother it might be good for her. And Roberta thought her sick mother would get a big bang out of[5] a dancing one. We got excited about it and curled each other's hair[6]. After breakfast we sat on the bed watching the road from the window. Roberta's socks were still wet. She washed them the night before and put them on the radiator to dry. They hadn't, but she put them on anyway because their tops[7] were so pretty—scalloped[8] in pink. Each of us had a purple construction-paper basket that we had made in craft class[9]. Mine had a yellow crayon rabbit[10] on it. Roberta's had eggs with wiggly[11] lines of color. Inside were cellophane grass and just the jelly beans[12] because I'd eaten the two marshmallow eggs[13] they gave us. The Big Bozo came herself to get us. Smiling she

---

1 **statecases:** meninas acolhidas • 2 **what with:** seja por • 3 **in time:** a tempo • 4 **the teachers' lounge:** sala dos professores • 5 **would get a big bang out of:** seria sacudida por • 6 **curled each other's hair:** enrolamos o cabelo uma da outra • 7 **tops:** parte de cima da roupa • 8 **scalloped:** debruada • 9 **craft class:** aula de artesanato • 10 **crayon rabbit:** um coelho desenhado com giz de cera • 11 **wiggly:** listras onduladas • 12 **jelly beans:** jujubas • 13 **marshmallow eggs:** ovos de chocolate com recheio de marshmallow

told us we looked very nice and to come downstairs. We were so surprised by the smile we'd never seen before, neither of us moved.

"Don't you want to see your mommies[1]?"

I stood up first and spilled[2] the jelly beans all over the floor. Bozo's smile disappeared while we scrambled to get the candy up off the floor[3] and put it back in the grass.

She escorted us[4] downstairs to the first floor, where the other girls were lining up[5] to file into[6] the chapel. A bunch of grown-ups[7] stood to one side. Viewers mostly. The old biddies[8] who wanted servants and the fags[9] who wanted company looking for children they might want to adopt. Once in a while a grandmother. Almost never anybody young or anybody whose face wouldn't scare you in the night. Because if any of the real orphans had young relatives they wouldn't be real orphans. I saw Mary right away[10]. She had on those green slacks[11] I hated and hated even more now because didn't she know we were going to chapel? And that fur[12] jacket with the pocket linings[13] so ripped[14] she had to pull to get her hands out of them. But her face was pretty like always, and she smiled and waved[15] like she was the little girl looking for her mother—not me.

I walked slowly, trying not to drop the jelly beans and hoping the paper handle[16] would hold[17]. I had to use my last Chiclet because by the time I finished cutting everything out, all the Elmer's[18] was gone. I am left-handed[19] and the scissors never

---

1 **mommies:** mamães • 2 **spilled:** derramei • 3 **we scrambled to get the candy up off the floor:** nos arrastamos para pegar os doces do chão • 4 **she escorted us:** ela nos acompanhou • 5 **were lining up:** faziam uma fila • 6 **to file into:** para entrar em fila • 7 **grown-ups:** adultos • 8 **old biddies:** velhas senhoras (pejorativo) • 9 **fags:** afeminados (pejorativo) • 10 **right away:** em seguida • 11 **slacks:** calças • 12 **fur:** de pele • 13 **linings:** forros • 14 **ripped:** rasgados • 15 **waved:** acenou • 16 **paper handle:** alça de papel • 17 **would hold:** aguentaria • 18 **Elmer's:** marca de cola • 19 **left-handed:** canhota

worked for me. It didn't matter[1], though; I might just as well have chewed the gum. Mary dropped to her knees and grabbed me, mashing[2] the basket, the jelly beans, and the grass into her ratty[3] fur jacket.

"Twyla, baby. Twyla, baby!"

I could have killed her. Already I heard the big girls in the orchard the next time saying, "Twyyyyyla, baby!" But I couldn't stay mad at Mary while she was smiling and hugging me and smelling of Lady Esther dusting powder[4]. I wanted to stay buried[5] in her fur all day.

To tell the truth I forgot about Roberta. Mary and I got in line for the traipse[6] into chapel and I was feeling proud because she looked so beautiful even in those ugly green slacks that made her behind stick out[7]. A pretty mother on earth is better than a beautiful dead one in the sky even if she did leave you all alone to go dancing.

I felt a tap[8] on my shoulder, turned, and saw Roberta smiling. I smiled back, but not too much lest[9] somebody think this visit was the biggest thing that ever happened in my life. Then Roberta said, "Mother, I want you to meet my roommate, Twyla. And that's Twyla's mother."

I looked up it seemed for miles. She was big. Bigger than any man and on her chest was the biggest cross I'd ever seen. I swear it was six inches long each way. And in the crook of her arm was[10] the biggest Bible ever made.

Mary, simple-minded as ever[11], grinned[12] and tried to yank

---

1 **it didn't matter:** não importava • 2 **mashing:** amassando • 3 **ratty:** puída; gasta • 4 **Lady Esther dusting power:** o pó de arroz da marca Lady Esther • 5 **buried:** enterrada • 6 **traipse:** lenta caminhada • 7 **made her behind stick out:** realçava seu traseiro • 8 **tap:** batidinha • 9 **lest:** para que ninguém • 10 **in the crook of her arm was:** e na dobra de seu braço segurava • 11 **simple-minded as ever:** ingênua como sempre • 12 **grinned:** sorriu

her hand out of the pocket[1] with the raggedy[2] lining—to shake hands, I guess. Roberta's mother looked down at me and then looked down at Mary too. She didn't say anything, just grabbed Roberta with her Bible-free hand and stepped out of line, walking quickly to the rear of it. Mary was still grinning because she's not too swift[3] when it comes to[4] what's really going on. Then this light bulb[5] goes off in her head and she says "That bitch[6]!" really loud and us almost in the chapel now. Organ music whining[7]; the Bonny Angels[8] singing sweetly. Everybody in the world turned around to look. And Mary would have kept it up[9]—kept calling names if I hadn't squeezed[10] her hand as hard as I could. That helped a little, but she still twitched[11] and crossed and uncrossed her legs all through service. Even groaned[12] a couple of times. Why did I think she would come there and act right? Slacks. No hat like the grandmothers and viewers, and groaning all the while[13]. When we stood for hymns she kept her mouth shut. Wouldn't even look at the words on the page. She actually reached in her purse[14] for a mirror to check her lipstick. All I could think of was that she really needed to be killed. The sermon lasted a year, and I knew the real orphans were looking smug[15] again.

We were supposed to have lunch in the teachers' lounge, but Mary didn't bring anything, so we picked fur and cellophane grass[16] off the mashed jelly beans and ate them. I could

---

1 **to yank her hand out of the pocket:** tentou tirar a mão do bolso • 2 **raggedy:** esfarrapado • 3 **swift:** rápida • 4 **when it comes to:** quando se trata de... • 5 **light bulb:** lâmpada • 6 **that bitch!:** aquela vadia! • 7 **whining:** como um lamento • 8 **Bonny Angels:** se refere ao coral Anjos de St. Bonaventure • 9 **would have kept it up:** teria continuado • 10 **hadn't squeezed:** se não tivesse apertado • 11 **twitched:** se contorceu • 12 **groaned:** gemeu • 13 **all the while:** o tempo todo • 14 **purse:** bolsa • 15 **were looking smug:** pareciam presunçosos • 16 **fur and cellophane grass:** pelos e fiapos de celofane

have killed her. I sneaked a look[1] at Roberta. Her mother had brought chicken legs[2] and ham sandwiches and oranges and a whole box of chocolate-covered grahams[3]. Roberta drank milk from a thermos while her mother read the Bible to her.

Things are not right. The wrong food is always with the wrong people. Maybe that's why I got into waitress work later —to match up[4] the right people with the right food. Roberta just let those chicken legs sit there, but she did bring a stack of[5] grahams up to me later when the visit was over. I think she was sorry that her mother would not shake my mother's hand[6]. And I liked that and I liked the fact that she didn't say a word about Mary groaning all the way through the service and not bringing any lunch.

Roberta left in May when the apple trees were heavy[7] and white. On her last day we went to the orchard to watch the big girls smoke and dance by the radio. It didn't matter that they said, "Twyyyyyla, baby." We sat on the ground and breathed. Lady Esther. Apple blossoms[8]. I still go soft[9] when I smell one or the other. Roberta was going home. The big cross and the big Bible was coming to get her and she seemed sort of glad and sort of not. I thought I would die in that room of four beds without her and I knew Bozo had plans to move some other dumped kid in there with me. Roberta promised to write every day, which was really sweet of her[10] because she couldn't read a lick[11] so how could she write anybody. I would have drawn pictures and sent them to her but she never gave me her

---

1 **I sneaked a look:** olhei dissimuladamente • 2 **chicken legs:** coxas de frango • 3 **grahams (crackers):** bolachas da marca Graham • 4 **to match up:** para combinar • 5 **a stack of:** um punhado de • 6 **would not shake my mother's hand:** não tinha apertado a mão da minha mãe • 7 **heavy:** carregadas • 8 **apple blossoms:** flores de macieira • 9 **I still go soft:** eu ainda me derreto • 10 **really sweet of her:** muito gentil da parte dela • 11 **she couldn't read a lick:** ela não conseguia ler nada

address. Little by little she faded[1]. Her wet socks with the pink scalloped tops and her big serious-looking eyes—that's all I could catch when I tried to bring her to mind[2].

I was working behind the counter[3] at the Howard Johnson's[4] on the Thruway[5] just before the Kingston exit. Not a bad job. Kind of a long ride[6] from Newburgh, but okay once I got there. Mine was the second night shift[7]—eleven to seven. Very light[8] until a Greyhound[9] checked in for breakfast around six-thirty. At that hour the sun was all the way clear of the hills behind the restaurant. The place looked better at night—more like shelter—but I loved it when the sun broke in[10], even if it did show all the cracks[11] in the vinyl and the speckled floor[12] looked dirty no matter what the mop boy[13] did.

It was August and a bus crowd was just unloading. They would stand around a long while: going to the john[14], and looking at gifts and junk-for-sale machines[15], reluctant[16] to sit down so soon. Even to eat. I was trying to fill the coffee pots and get them all situated on the electric burners[17] when I saw her. She was sitting in a booth[18] smoking a cigarette with two guys smothered in[19] head and facial hair. Her own hair was so big and wild I could hardly see her face. But the eyes. I would know them anywhere[20]. She had on a powder-blue halter[21]

---

1 **little by little she faded:** pouco a pouco ela foi se apagando da minha memória • 2 **to bring her to mind:** lembrar dela • 3 **counter:** balcão • 4 **Howard Johnson's:** cadeia de hotéis e restaurantes • 5 **Thruway:** via expressa • 6 **kind of a long ride:** um trajeto meio longo • 7 **shift:** turno • 8 **light:** tranquilo • 9 **Greyhound:** empresa de ônibus • 10 **broke in:** invadia • 11 **cracks:** rachaduras • 12 **speckled:** o chão manchado • 13 **mop boy:** o rapaz da limpeza • 14 **john:** banheiro • 15 **junk-for-sale machines:** máquinas automáticas que vendem bugigangas • 16 **reluctant:** reticentes • 17 **electric burners:** fogões elétricos • 18 **booth:** bancos acolchoados típicos das lanchonetes americanas • 19 **smothered in:** cobertos por • 20 **I would know them anywhere:** eu os reconheceria em qualquer parte • 21 **powder-blue halter:** corpete azul-claro

and shorts outfit and earrings¹ the size of bracelets. Talk about lipstick and eyebrow pencil. She made the big girls look like nuns². I couldn't get off the counter until seven o'clock, but I kept watching the booth in case they got up to leave before that. My replacement was on time³ for a change⁴, so I counted and stacked my receipts as fast as I could and signed off⁵. I walked over to the booths, smiling and wondering if she would remember me. Or even if she wanted to remember me. Maybe she didn't want to be reminded of St. Bonny's or to have anybody know she was ever there. I know I never talked about it to anybody.

I put my hands in my apron⁶ pockets and leaned against the back of the booth facing them.

"Roberta? Roberta Fisk?"

She looked up. "Yeah?"

"Twyla."

She squinted⁷ for a second and then said, "Wow."

"Remember me?"

"Sure. Hey. Wow."

"It's been a while," I said, and gave a smile to the two hairy guys.

"Yeah. Wow. You work here?"

"Yeah," I said. "I live in Newburgh."

"Newburgh? No kidding⁸?" She laughed then a private laugh that included the guys but only the guys, and they laughed with her. What could I do but laugh too and wonder why I was standing there with my knees showing out⁹ from under that uniform. Without looking I could see the blue and

---

1 **earrings:** brincos • 2 **nuns:** freiras • 3 **on time:** pontual • 4 **for a change:** para variar • 5 **signed off:** bati o ponto • 6 **apron:** avental • 7 **she squinted:** deixou os olhos entreabertos • 8 **no kidding?:** sério? • 9 **showing out:** à mostra

white triangle on my head, my hair shapeless in a net¹, my ankles thick² in white oxfords³. Nothing could have been less sheer⁴ than my stockings⁵. There was this silence that came down right after I laughed. A silence it was her turn to fill up. With introductions⁶, maybe, to her boyfriends or an invitation to sit down and have a Coke. Instead she lit a cigarette off the one she'd just finished and said, "We're on our way to the Coast. He's got an appointment with Hendrix."

She gestured casually toward the boy next to her.

"Hendrix? Fantastic," I said. "Really fantastic. What's she doing now?"

Roberta coughed⁷ on her cigarette and the two guys rolled their eyes up at the ceiling."

Hendrix. Jimi Hendrix, asshole⁸. He's only the biggest— Oh, wow. Forget it."

I was dismissed⁹ without anyone saying goodbye, so I thought I would do it for her.

"How's your mother?" I asked. Her grin cracked her whole face. She swallowed¹⁰. "Fine," she said. "How's yours?"

"Pretty as a picture," I said and turned away. The backs of my knees were damp¹¹. Howard Johnson's really was a dump¹² in the sunlight.

James is as comfortable as a house slipper¹³. He liked my cooking and I liked his big loud family. They have lived in

---

1 **shapeless in a net:** sem forma recolhido em uma rede • 2 **thick:** inchado • 3 **oxfords:** sapatos de cadarço • 4 **sheer:** transparente • 5 **stockings:** meia-calça • 6 **introductions:** apresentações • 7 **coughed:** tossiu • 8 **asshole:** imbecil • 9 **I was dismissed:** fui dispensada • 10 **she swallowed:** engoliu saliva • 11 **damp:** suadas • 12 **dump:** um muquifo • 13 **slipper:** pantufa

Newburgh all of their lives and talk about it the way people do who have always known a home. His grandmother is a porch swing older[1] than his father and when they talk about streets and avenues and buildings they call them names they no longer have. They still call the A & P[2] Rico's because it stands on[3] property once a mom and pop store[4] owned by Mr. Rico. And they call the new community college[5] Town Hall[6] because it once was. My mother-in-law puts up jelly[7] and cucumbers and buys butter wrapped in cloth from a dairy[8]. James and his father talk about fishing and baseball and I can see them all together on the Hudson[9] in a raggedy skiff[10]. Half the population of Newburgh is on welfare[11] now, but to my husband's family it was still some upstate paradise of a time long past. A time of ice houses[12] and vegetable wagons[13], coal furnaces[14] and children weeding[15] gardens. When our son was born my mother-in-law gave me the crib blanket[16] that had been hers.

But the town they remembered had changed. Something quick was in the air. Magnificent old houses, so ruined they had become shelter[17] for squatters[18] and rent risks[19], were bought and renovated. Smart IBM people moved out of their suburbs[20] back into the city and put shutters[21] up and herb gardens[22] in their backyards. A brochure[23] came in the mail announcing

---

1 **a porch swing older:** só um pouco mais velha • 2 **A & P:** cadeia de supermercados • 3 **it stands on:** se encontra • 4 **mom and pop store:** loja familiar • 5 **community college:** faculdade local • 6 **Town Hall:** prefeitura • 7 **jelly:** geleia • 8 **dairy:** leiteria • 9 **Hudson:** o rio Hudson • 10 **in a raggedy skiff:** em um esquife velho • 11 **is on welfare:** recebe ajuda do governo • 12 **ice houses:** fábricas de gelo • 13 **vegetable wagons:** carrinhos de verduras • 14 **coal furnaces:** fornos de carvão • 15 **weeding:** capinando • 16 **crib blanket:** cobertor de berço • 17 **shelter:** abrigo • 18 **squatters:** sem-teto • 19 **rent risks:** casas em mau estado (por isso era arriscado alugá-las) • 20 **suburbs:** bairros residenciais • 21 **shutters:** venezianas • 22 **herb gardens:** jardins de ervas e temperos • 23 **brochure:** folheto

the opening of a Food Emporium[1]. Gourmet food it said—and listed items the rich IBM crowd would want. It was located in a new mall[2] at the edge of town and I drove out to shop there one day—just to see. It was late in June. After the tulips were gone and the Queen Elizabeth roses were open everywhere. I railed my cart along the aisle[3] tossing in smoked oysters and Robert's sauce[4] and things I knew would sit in my cupboard for years. Only when I found some Klondike[5] ice cream bars did I feel less guilty about spending James's fireman's salary so foolishly. My father-in-law ate them with the same gusto[6] little Joseph did.

Waiting in the check-out line[7] I heard a voice say, "Twyla!"

The classical music piped[8] over the aisles had affected me and the woman leaning toward me[9] was dressed to kill[10]. Diamonds on her hand, a smart white summer dress. "I'm Mrs. Benson," I said.

"Ho. Ho. The Big Bozo," she sang.

For a split second[11] I didn't know what she was talking about. She had a bunch of asparagus and two cartons of fancy water.

"Roberta!"

"Right."

"For heaven's sake. Roberta."

"You look great," she said.

"So do you[12]. Where are you? Here? In Newburgh?"

"Yes. Over in Annandale."

---

1 **Food Emporium:** rede de supermercados • 2 **mall:** *shopping* • 3 **I railed my cart along the aisle:** eu empurrei o carrinho pelo corredor • 4 **tossing in smoked oysters and Robert's sauce:** enchendo-o com ostras defumadas e molho de mostarda • 5 **Klondike:** marca de sorvete de creme coberto com chocolate • 6 **gusto:** entusiasmo • 7 **check-out line:** na fila do caixa • 8 **piped:** que soava • 9 **leaning toward me:** se inclinando na minha direção • 10 **was dressed to kill:** vestida para matar • 11 **for a split second:** durante uma fração de segundo • 12 **so do you:** você também

I was opening my mouth to say more when the cashier called my attention to her empty counter.

"Meet you outside." Roberta pointed her finger and went into the express line.

I placed the groceries and kept myself from glancing around[1] to check Roberta's progress. I remembered Howard Johnson's and looking for a chance to speak only to be greeted with a stingy[2] "wow." But she was waiting for me and her huge hair was sleek[3] now, smooth around a small, nicely shaped head. Shoes, dress, everything lovely and summery[4] and rich. I was dying to know[5] what happened to her, how she got from Jimi Hendrix to Annandale, a neighborhood full of doctors and IBM executives. Easy, I thought. Everything is so easy for them. They think they own the world.

"How long," I asked her. "How long have you been here?"

"A year. I got married to a man who lives here. And you, you're married too, right? Benson, you said."

"Yeah. James Benson."

"And is he nice?"

"Oh, is he nice?"

"Well, is he?" Roberta's eyes were steady[6] as though she really meant the question[7] and wanted an answer.

"He's wonderful, Roberta. Wonderful."

"So you're happy."

"Very."

"That's good," she said and nodded her head. "I always hoped you'd be happy. Any kids? I know you have kids."

---

1 **kept myself from glancing around:** evitei olhar em volta • 2 **stingy:** lacônico • 3 **sleek:** liso • 4 **summery:** típico do verão; estival • 5 **I was dying to know:** estava morrendo de vontade de saber • 6 **Roberta's eyes were steady:** os olhos de Roberta me olhavam fixamente • 7 **as though she really meant the question:** como se ela realmente quisesse saber

"One. A boy. How about you?"

"Four."

"Four?"

She laughed. "Step kids[1]. He's a widower[2]."

"Oh."

"Got a minute? Let's have a coffee."

I thought about the Klondikes melting[3] and the inconvenience of going all the way to my car and putting the bags in the trunk[4]. Served me right[5] for buying all that stuff I didn't need. Roberta was ahead of me[6].

"Put them in my car. It's right here."

And then I saw the dark blue limousine.

"You married a Chinaman[7]?"

"No," she laughed. "He's the driver."

"Oh, my. If the Big Bozo could see you now."

We both giggled[8]. Really giggled. Suddenly, in just a pulse beat[9], twenty years disappeared and all of it came rushing back. The big girls (whom we called gar girls[10]—Roberta's misheard word[11] for the evil stone faces described in a civics class) there dancing in the orchard, the ploppy[12] mashed potatoes, the double weenies, the Spam with pineapple. We went into the coffee shop holding onto one another and I tried to think why we were glad to see each other this time and not before. Once, twelve years ago, we passed like strangers. A black girl and a white girl meeting in a Howard Johnson's on the road and having nothing to say. One in a blue and white triangle waitress

---

1 **step kids:** enteados • 2 **widower:** viúvo • 3 **melting:** derretendo • 4 **trunk:** porta-malas • 5 **served me right:** bem-feito; merecido • 6 **Roberta was ahead of me:** Roberta se adiantou • 7 **Chinaman:** chinês • 8 **giggled:** demos uma risadinha • 9 **in just a pulse beat:** num piscar de olhos • 10 **gar girls (gargoyles):** gárgulas • 11 **Roberta's misheard word:** uma palavra que Roberta entendeu errado • 12 **ploppy:** pastoso

hat—the other on her way to see, Hendrix. Now we were behaving like sisters separated for much too long. Those four short months were nothing in time. Maybe it was the thing itself. Just being there, together. Two little girls who knew what nobody else in the world knew—how not to ask questions. How to believe what had to be believed. There was politeness in that reluctance[1] and generosity as well. Is your mother sick too? No, she dances all night. Oh—and an understanding nod.

We sat in a booth by the window and fell into recollection[2] like veterans.

"Did you ever learn to read?"

"Watch." She picked up the menu. "Special of the day. Cream of corn[3] soup. Entrees[4]. Two dots and a wriggly line[5]. Quiche. Chef salad, scallops[6] . . ."

I was laughing and applauding when the waitress came up.

"Remember the Easter baskets[7]?"

"And how we tried to introduce them?"

"Your mother with that cross like two telephone poles."

"And yours with those tight[8] slacks."

We laughed so loudly heads turned and made the laughter harder to suppress[9].

"What happened to the Jimi Hendrix date?"

Roberta made a blow-out sound with her lips[10].

"When he died I thought about you."

"Oh, you heard about him finally?"

---

1 **there was politeness in that reluctance:** havia educação naquela relutância • 2 **fell into recollection:** mergulhamos em lembranças • 3 **corn:** milho • 4 **entrees:** entradas (culinária) • 5 **two dots and a wriggly line:** dois pontos e uma linha torta • 6 **scallops:** vieiras • 7 **Easter baskets:** cestas de Páscoa • 8 **tight:** justas • 9 **harder to suppress:** mais difícil de conter • 10 **made a blow-out sound with her lips:** soprou ruidosamente

"Finally. Come on, I was a small-town country waitress[1]."

"And I was a small-town country dropout[2]. God, were we wild. I still don't know how I got out of there alive[3]."

"But you did."

"I did. I really did. Now I'm Mrs. Kenneth Norton."

"Sounds like a mouthful[4]."

"It is."

"Servants and all?"

Roberta held up[5] two fingers.

"Ow! What does he do?"

"Computers and stuff. What do I know?"

"I don't remember a hell of a lot from those days, but Lord, St. Bonny's is as clear as daylight. Remember Maggie? The day she fell down and those gar girls laughed at her?"

Roberta looked up from her salad and stared at me[6]. "Maggie didn't fall," she said.

"Yes, she did. You remember."

"No, Twyla. They knocked her down[7]. Those girls pushed her down and tore[8] her clothes. In the orchard."

"I don't—that's not what happened."

"Sure it is. In the orchard. Remember how scared we were?"

"Wait a minute. I don't remember any of that."

"And Bozo was fired[9]."

"You're crazy. She was there when I left. You left before me."

"I went back. You weren't there when they fired Bozo."

"What?"

---

1 **a small-town country waitress:** uma garçonete de cidade pequena • 2 **dropout:** pessoa que abandona os estudos ou hábitos convencionais • 3 **how I got out of there alive:** como saí de lá viva • 4 **sounds like a mouthful:** parece ser um partidão • 5 **held up:** levantou • 6 **stared at me:** me olhou fixamente • 7 **they knocked her down:** elas derrubaram no chão • 8 **tore:** rasgaram • 9 **was fired:** foi demitida

"Twice. Once for a year when I was about ten, another for two months when I was fourteen. That's when I ran away[1]."

"You ran away from St. Bonny's?"

"I had to. What do you want? Me dancing in that orchard?"

"Are you sure about Maggie?"

"Of course I'm sure. You've blocked it, Twyla. It happened. Those girls had behavior problems, you know."

"Didn't they, though. But why can't I remember the Maggie thing?"

"Believe me. It happened. And we were there."

"Who did you room with when you went back?" I asked her as if I would know her. The Maggie thing was troubling me[2].

"Creeps[3]. They tickled themselves[4] in the night."

My ears were itching[5] and I wanted to go home suddenly. This was all very well but she couldn't just comb her hair, wash her face and pretend everything was hunky-dory[6]. After the Howard Johnson's snub[7]. And no apology. Nothing.

"Were you on dope[8] or what that time at Howard Johnson's?" I tried to make my voice sound friendlier than I felt.

"Maybe, a little. I never did drugs much. Why?"

"I don't know; you acted sort of like you didn't want to know me then."

"Oh, Twyla, you know how it was in those days: black-white. You know how everything was."

But I didn't know. I thought it was just the opposite.

---

1 **I ran away:** eu fugi • 2 **was troubling me:** me perturbava • 3 **creeps:** nojentas • 4 **they tickled themselves:** elas se tocavam à noite • 5 **my ears were itching:** me incomodava ouvir aquilo (minhas orelhas coçavam) • 6 **everything was hunky-dory:** tudo estava certo • 7 **snub:** humilhação • 8 **were you on dope...?:** você estava drogada?

Busloads[1] of blacks and whites came into Howard Johnson's together. They roamed together[2] then: students, musicians, lovers, protesters. You got to see everything at Howard Johnson's and blacks were very friendly with whites in those days. But sitting there with nothing on my plate but two hard tomato wedges[3] wondering about the melting Klondikes it seemed childish remembering the slight[4]. We went to her car, and with the help of the driver, got my stuff into my station wagon[5].

"We'll keep in touch this time," she said.

"Sure," I said. "Sure. Give me a call."

"I will," she said, and then just as I was sliding behind the wheel[6], she leaned into the window. "By the way. Your mother. Did she ever stop dancing?"

I shook my head. "No. Never."

Roberta nodded.

"And yours? Did she ever get well?"

She smiled a tiny[7] sad smile. "No. She never did. Look, call me, okay?"

"Okay," I said, but I knew I wouldn't. Roberta had messed up[8] my past somehow with that business about Maggie. I wouldn't forget a thing like that. Would I?

Strife[9] came to us that fall. At least that's what the paper called it. Strife. Racial strife. The word made me think of a bird—a big shrieking[10] bird out of 1,000,000,000 B.C. Flapping its wings[11] and cawing[12]. Its eye with no lid[13] always bearing down

---

1 **busloads:** vários, montes • 2 **they roamed together:** eles andavam juntos • 3 **wedges:** pedaços • 4 **slight:** desfeita • 5 **station wagon:** perua • 6 **just as I was sliding behind the wheel:** quando sentei atrás do volante • 7 **tiny:** minúsculo • 8 **had messed up:** tinha estragado • 9 **strife:** conflito (racial) • 10 **shrieking:** guinchando • 11 **flapping its wings:** batendo as asas • 12 **cawing:** grasnando • 13 **lid:** pálpebra

on you¹. All day it screeched² and at night it slept on the rooftops³. It woke you in the morning and from the Today show⁴ to the eleven o'clock news it kept you an awful company. I couldn't figure it out⁵ from one day to the next. I knew I was supposed to feel something strong, but I didn't know what, and James wasn't any help. Joseph was on the list of kids to be transferred from the junior high school to another one at some far-out-of-the-way place and I thought it was a good thing until I heard it was a bad thing. I mean I didn't know. All the schools seemed dumps to me, and the fact that one was nicer looking didn't hold much weight⁶. But the papers⁷ were full of it and then the kids began to get jumpy⁸. In August, mind you⁹. Schools weren't even open yet. I thought Joseph might be frightened to go over there, but he didn't seem scared so I forgot about it, until I found myself driving along Hudson Street out there by the school they were trying to integrate and saw a line of women marching. And who do you suppose was in line, big as life, holding a sign¹⁰ in front of her bigger than her mother's cross? MOTHERS HAVE RIGHTS TOO! it said.

I drove on¹¹, and then changed my mind. I circled the block¹², slowed down, and honked my horn¹³.

Roberta looked over and when she saw me she waved. I didn't wave back, but I didn't move either. She handed her sign to another woman and came over¹⁴ to where I was parked.

---

1 **bearing down on you:** sempre observando você • 2 **it screeched:** ele gritava • 3 **rooftops:** telhados • 4 **the Today show:** programa de notícias matinal da rede NBC • 5 **I couldn't figure it out:** eu não percebia a diferença • 6 **didn't hold much weight:** não fazia muita diferença • 7 **the papers:** os jornais • 8 **jumpy:** nervosas • 9 **in August, mind you:** era agosto, porém • 10 **sign:** cartaz • 11 **I drove on:** segui dirigindo • 12 **I circled the block:** dei a volta no quarteirão • 13 **honked my horn:** toquei minha buzina • 14 **came over:** veio até

"Hi."

"What are you doing?"

"Picketing[1]. What's it look like?"

"What for[2]?"

"What do you mean, 'What for?' They want to take my kids and send them out of the neighborhood. They don't want to go."

"So what if they go to another school? My boy's being bussed too[3], and I don't mind. Why should you?"

"It's not about us, Twyla. Me and you. It's about our kids."

"What's more us than that[4]?"

"Well, it is a free country."

"Not yet, but it will be."

"What the hell does that mean? I'm not doing anything to you."

"You really think that?"

"I know it."

"I wonder what made me think you were different."

"I wonder what made me think you were different."

"Look at them," I said. "Just look. Who do they think they are? Swarming[5] all over the place like they own it[6]. And now they think they can decide where my child goes to school. Look at them, Roberta. They're Bozos."

Roberta turned around and looked at the women. Almost all of them were standing still[7] now, waiting. Some were even edging toward us[8]. Roberta looked at me out of some refrigerator behind her eyes. "No, they're not. They're just mothers."

---

1 **picketing:** manifestando • 2 **what for?:** para quê? • 3 **my boy's being bussed too:** meu filho também foi transferido • 4 **what's more us than that?:** o que é mais nosso do que isso? • 5 **swarming:** lotando • 6 **like they own it:** como se pertencesse a elas • 7 **were standing still:** estavam paradas • 8 **edging toward us:** avançando em nossa direção

"And what am I? Swiss cheese?"
"I used to curl your hair."
"I hated your hands in my hair."

The women were moving. Our faces looked mean to them of course and they looked as though they could not wait to throw themselves in front of a police car, or better yet, into my car and drag me away by my ankles[1]. Now they surrounded my car and gently, gently began to rock it[2]. I swayed[3] back and forth like a sideways yo-yo. Automatically I reached for Roberta[4], like the old days in the orchard when they saw us watching them and we had to get out of there, and if one of us fell the other pulled her up and if one of us was caught the other stayed to kick and scratch[5], and neither would leave the other behind. My arm shot out of the car window but no receiving hand was there. Roberta was looking at me sway from side to side in the car and her face was still[6]. My purse slid from the car seat down under the dashboard[7]. The four policemen who had been drinking Tab[8] in their car finally got the message and strolled over[9], forcing their way through[10] the women. Quietly, firmly they spoke. "Okay, ladies. Back in line or off the streets."

Some of them went away willingly[11]; others had to be urged away[12] from the car doors and the hood[13]. Roberta didn't move. She was looking steadily at me. I was fumbling to turn on the

---

1 **drag me away by my ankles:** me arrastar pelos tornozelos • 2 **to rock it:** sacudi-lo • 3 **I swayed:** balancei • 4 **I reached for Roberta:** estendi a mão para Roberta • 5 **to kick and scratch:** chutar e arranhar • 6 **her face was still:** seu rosto permaneceu impassível • 7 **dashboard:** painel • 8 **Tab:** bebida de cola light • 9 **strolled over:** e se aproximaram sem pressa • 10 **forcing their way through:** abrindo caminho à força • 11 **willingly:** por vontade própria • 12 **others had to be urged away:** outras tiveram que ser forçadas a sair • 13 **hood:** capô

ignition[1], which wouldn't catch because the gearshift[2] was still in drive. The seats of the car were a mess[3] because the swaying[4] had thrown my grocery coupons all over it and my purse was sprawled[5] on the floor.

"Maybe I am different now, Twyla. But you're not. You're the same little state kid who kicked a poor old black lady when she was down on the ground. You kicked a black lady and you have the nerve[6] to call me a bigot[7]."

The coupons were everywhere and the guts of my purse[8] were bunched[9] under the dashboard. What was she saying? Black? Maggie wasn't black.

"She wasn't black," I said.

"Like hell she wasn't, and you kicked her. We both did. You kicked a black lady who couldn't even scream."

"Liar!"

"You're the liar! Why don't you just go on home and leave us alone, huh?"

She turned away and I skidded away from the curb[10].

The next morning I went into the garage and cut the side out of the carton our portable TV had come in. It wasn't nearly big enough, but after a while I had a decent sign: red spray-painted letters on a white background[11]—AND SO DO CHILDREN[12]. I meant just to go down[13] to the school and tack it up[14]

---

1 **I was fumbling to turn on the ignition:** tentava ligar o motor de forma desajeitada • 2 **gearshift:** alavanca de câmbio • 3 **mess:** bagunça • 4 **swaying:** sacudida • 5 **sprawled:** esparramada • 6 **you have the nerve:** tem a ousadia • 7 **bigot:** fanática; intolerante • 8 **the guts of my purse:** o conteúdo da minha bolsa • 9 **bunched:** amontoados • 10 **I skidded away from the curb:** saí derrapando para longe do meio-fio • 11 **background:** fundo • 12 **and so do children:** e as crianças também • 13 **I meant just to go down:** eu só pretendia ir • 14 **tack it up:** pendurá-lo

somewhere so those cows[1] on the picket line across the street could see it, but when I got there, some ten or so others had already assembled—protesting the cows across the street. Police permits[2] and everything. I got in line and we strutted[3] in time on our side while Roberta's group strutted on theirs. That first day we were all dignified, pretending the other side didn't exist. The second day there was name calling[4] and finger gestures. But that was about all. People changed signs from time to time, but Roberta never did and neither did I[5]. Actually my sign didn't make sense without Roberta's. "And so do children what?" one of the women on my side asked me. Have rights, I said, as though it was obvious.

Roberta didn't acknowledge[6] my presence in any way and I got to thinking[7] maybe she didn't know I was there. I began to pace[8] myself in the line, jostling[9] people one minute and lagging behind[10] the next, so Roberta and I could reach the end of our respective lines at the same time and there would be a moment in our turn when we would face each other. Still[11], I couldn't tell whether she saw me and knew my sign was for her. The next day I went early before we were scheduled to assemble[12]. I waited until she got there before I exposed my new creation. As soon as she hoisted[13] her MOTHERS HAVE RIGHTS TOO! I began to wave my new one, which said, HOW WOULD YOU KNOW? I know she saw that one, but I had gotten addicted now. My signs got crazier each day, and the women on my side

---

1 **cows:** vacas • 2 **police permits:** permissão da polícia • 3 **we strutted:** marchamos • 4 **name calling:** insultos • 5 **neither did I:** eu também não • 6 **didn't acknowledge:** não se deu conta • 7 **I got to thinking:** comecei a pensar • 8 **to pace:** caminhar • 9 **jostling:** empurrando • 10 **lagging behind:** ficando para trás • 11 **still:** ainda assim • 12 **we were scheduled to assemble:** tínhamos marcado de nos reunir • 13 **she hoisted:** ela levantou

decided that I was a kook¹. They couldn't make heads or tails out of my brilliant screaming posters².

I brought a painted sign in queenly³ red with huge black letters that said, IS YOUR MOTHER WELL? Roberta took her lunch break and didn't come back for the rest of the day or any day after. Two days later I stopped going too and couldn't have been missed⁴ because nobody understood my signs anyway.

It was a nasty⁵ six weeks. Classes were suspended and Joseph didn't go to anybody's school until October. The children—everybody's children—soon got bored with that extended vacation they thought was going to be so great. They looked at TV until their eyes flattened⁶. I spent a couple of mornings tutoring⁷ my son, as the other mothers said we should. Twice I opened a text from last year that he had never turned in⁸. Twice he yawned⁹ in my face. Other mothers organized living room sessions so the kids would keep up¹⁰. None of the kids could concentrate so they drifted back¹¹ to The Price Is Right¹² and The Brady Bunch¹³. When the school finally opened there were fights once or twice and some sirens roared¹⁴ through the streets every once in a while. There were a lot of photographers from Albany¹⁵. And just when ABC¹⁶ was about to send up a news crew¹⁷, the kids settled down¹⁸ like nothing in the

---

1 **kook:** louca • 2 **they couldn't make heads or tails out of my brilliant screaming posters:** não conseguiam entender meus cartazes berrantes e geniais sem pé nem cabeça • 3 **queenly:** majestoso • 4 **couldn't have been missed:** minha ausência não foi sentida • 5 **nasty:** desagradáveis • 6 **until their eyes flattened:** até seus olhos secarem • 7 **tutoring:** dando aulas • 8 **he had never turned in:** que ele nunca havia entregado • 9 **he yawned:** ele bocejou • 10 **would keep up:** não perdessem o ritmo • 11 **they drifted back:** voltaram pouco a pouco • 12 **The Price is Right:** programa de auditório com competição • 13 **The Brady Bunch:** série de televisão norte-americana • 14 **some sirens roared:** algumas sirenes tocaram • 15 **Albany:** capital do estado de Nova York • 16 **ABC:** rede de televisão • 17 **news crew:** equipe de jornalistas • 18 **settled down:** acalmaram-se

world had happened. Joseph hung my HOW WOULD YOU KNOW? sign in his bedroom. I don't know what became of AND SO DO CHILDREN. I think my father-in-law cleaned some fish on it. He was always puttering around[1] in our garage. Each of his five children lived in Newburgh and he acted as though he had five extra homes.

I couldn't help looking for Roberta when Joseph graduated from high school, but I didn't see her. It didn't trouble me[2] much what she had said to me in the car. I mean the kicking part. I know I didn't do that, I couldn't do that. But I was puzzled by her telling me Maggie was black. When I thought about it I actually couldn't be certain. She wasn't pitch-black[3], I knew, or I would have remembered that. What I remember was the kiddie hat[4], and the semicircle legs. I tried to reassure myself about the race thing[5] for a long time until it dawned on me[6] that the truth was already there, and Roberta knew it. I didn't kick her; I didn't join in[7] with the gar girls and kick that lady, but I sure did want to. We watched and never tried to help her and never called for help. Maggie was my dancing mother. Deaf, I thought, and dumb. Nobody inside. Nobody who would hear you if you cried in the night. Nobody who could tell you anything important that you could use. Rocking, dancing, swaying as she walked. And when the gar girls pushed her down, and started roughhousing[8], I knew she wouldn't scream, couldn't—just like me and I was glad about that.

---

1 **puttering around:** mexendo • 2 **it didn't trouble me:** não me incomodava • 3 **pitch-black:** negra como o piche • 4 **kiddie hat:** gorro de criança • 5 **I tried to reassure myself about the race thing:** eu tentei me convencer sobre o assunto da raça • 6 **it dawned on me:** até que me dei conta • 7 **I didn't join in:** não me juntei • 8 **roughhousing:** agir de modo violento

We decided not to have a tree, because Christmas would be at my mother-in-law's house, so why have a tree at both places? Joseph was at SUNY New Paltz[1] and we had to economize, we said. But at the last minute, I changed my mind. Nothing could be that bad. So I rushed around town[2] looking for a tree, something small but wide. By the time I found a place, it was snowing and very late. I dawdled[3] like it was the most important purchase[4] in the world and the tree man was fed up with me[5]. Finally I chose one and had it tied onto the trunk of the car. I drove away slowly because the sand trucks were not out yet[6] and the streets could be murder[7] at the beginning of a snowfall[8]. Downtown the streets were wide and rather empty except for a cluster[9] of people coming out of the Newburgh Hotel. The one hotel in town that wasn't built out of cardboard[10] and Plexiglas. A party, probably. The men huddled[11] in the snow were dressed in tails[12] and the women had on furs[13]. Shiny things glittered[14] from underneath their coats. It made me tired to look at them. Tired, tired, tired. On the next corner was a small diner[15] with loops and loops of paper bells[16] in the window. I stopped the car and went in. Just for a cup of coffee and twenty minutes of peace before I went home and tried to finish everything before Christmas Eve.

"Twyla?"

---

1 **SUNY New Paltz:** Universidade do Estado de Nova York em New Paltz • 2 **I rushed around town:** corri por toda a cidade • 3 **I dawdled:** me dei tempo • 4 **purchase:** compra • 5 **fed up with me:** farto de mim • 6 **the sand trucks were not out yet:** os caminhões de areia (para evitar derrapagens) ainda não haviam saído • 7 **the streets could be murder:** as ruas podiam ser mortais • 8 **snowfall:** nevada • 9 **cluster:** aglomerado • 10 **cardboard:** cartolina • 11 **huddled:** apinhados • 12 **dressed in tails:** vestiam fraques • 13 **had on furs:** vestiam peles • 14 **glittered:** brilhavam • 15 **diner:** lanchonete • 16 **loops and loops of paper bells:** tiras e tiras de sinos de papel

There she was. In a silvery evening gown[1] and dark fur coat. A man and another woman were with her, the man fumbling for change to put in the cigarette machine. The woman was humming and tapping on the counter with her fingernails[2]. They all looked a little bit drunk.

"Well. It's you."

"How are you?"

I shrugged[3]. "Pretty good. Frazzled[4]. Christmas and all."

"Regular?" called the woman from the counter.

"Fine," Roberta called back and then, "Wait for me in the car."

She slipped into the booth beside me. "I have to tell you something, Twyla. I made up my mind[5] if I ever saw you again, I'd tell you."

"I'd just as soon not hear anything[6], Roberta. It doesn't matter now, anyway."

"No," she said. "Not about that."

"Don't be long[7]," said the woman. She carried two regulars to go and the man peeled his cigarette pack[8] as they left.

"It's about St. Bonny's and Maggie."

"Oh, please."

"Listen to me. I really did think she was black. I didn't make that up[9]. I really thought so. But now I can't be sure. I just remember her as old, so old. And because she couldn't talk—

---

1 **silvery evening gown:** em um vestido de festa prateado • 2 **humming and tapping on the counter with her fingernails:** cantando baixinho e batendo com as unhas sobre o balcão • 3 **I shrugged:** encolhi os ombros • 4 **frazzled:** exausta (coloquial) • 5 **I made up my mind:** decidi • 6 **I'd just as soon not hear anything:** eu preferiria não ouvir nada • 7 **don't be long:** não se demore • 8 **peeled his cigarette pack:** ele tirou o celofane do maço de cigarro • 9 **I didn't make that up:** eu não inventei aquilo

well, you know, I thought she was crazy. She'd been brought up[1] in an institution like my mother was and like I thought I would be too. And you were right. We didn't kick her. It was the gar girls. Only them. But, well, I wanted to. I really wanted them to hurt her[2]. I said we did it, too. You and me, but that's not true. And I don't want you to carry that around[3]. It was just that I wanted to do it so bad[4] that day—wanting to is doing it."

Her eyes were watery[5] from the drinks she'd had, I guess. I know it's that way with me. One glass of wine and I start bawling[6] over the littlest thing.

"We were kids, Roberta."

"Yeah. Yeah. I know, just kids."

"Eight."

"Eight."

"And lonely."

"Scared, too."

She wiped[7] her cheeks with the heel of her hand[8] and smiled.

"Well that's all I wanted to say."

I nodded and couldn't think of any way to fill the silence that went from the diner past the paperbells on out into the snow. It was heavy now[9]. I thought I'd better wait for the sand trucks before starting home.

"Thanks, Roberta."

"Sure."

---

1 **she'd been brought up:** tinha sido criada • 2 **to hurt her:** que a machucassem • 3 **I don't want you to carry that around:** eu não quero que você carregue isso consigo • 4 **I wanted to do it so bad:** eu tinha tanta vontade de fazê-lo • 5 **watery:** lacrimejantes • 6 **bawling:** choramingar • 7 **she wiped:** secou • 8 **the heel of her hand:** com a base de sua mão • 9 **it was heavy now:** nevava forte agora

"Did I tell you my mother, she never did stop dancing."

"Yes. You told me. And mine, she never got well." Roberta lifted her hands from the tabletop[1] and covered her face with her palms. When she took them away[2] she really was crying. "Oh shit, Twyla. Shit, shit, shit. What the hell happened to Maggie?"

---

1 **lifted her hands from the tabletop:** levantou as mãos de cima da mesa
2 **when she took them away:** quando ela as afastou

Doris Lessing

To Room Nineteen

"This is a story, I suppose, about a failure in intelligence: the Rawlingses' marriage was grounded in intelligence."

BIOGRAFIA
Doris Lessing

Doris May Tayler (Kermanshah, Irã, 1919) cresceu no Zimbábue, sob o jugo asfixiante de uma mãe para quem a casa sempre foi seu pequeno reino. Naquela época, o Zimbábue se chamava Rodésia e era uma colônia inglesa. Doris tinha seis anos quando a sua família se instalou ali, atraída pelas promessas de fazer fortuna cultivando milho e tabaco. Seu pai, que tinha lutado na Primeira Guerra Mundial, chegou despedaçado a seu novo lar. Doris passava as tardes com seu irmão Henry, ambos fascinados pela natureza selvagem do lugar. Com 13 anos, deixou o colégio e começou a trabalhar como ama-seca para poder se tornar independente, já que não se dava nada bem com a sua mãe. E as coisas não iam bem. Então começou a escrever, para escapar de um mundo disposto a aniquilá-la. Conseguiu publicar dois contos em uma revista sul-africana, e com o que havia poupado trabalhando, comprou uma passagem de ida para Salisbury (a capital do Zimbábue, atual Harare). Tinha 18 anos. O que encontrou em Salisbury foi outro trabalho terrível, agora como telefonista.

Alguns anos depois, em 1939, conseguiu fugir de tudo isso casando com um funcionário público, Frank Wisdom. Tiveram dois filhos até que um dia Doris saiu de casa. Wisdom pediu o divórcio. A sua mulher tinha se aliado aos comunistas. Corria o ano de 1943, e Doris deixava para trás seus dois filhos, que voltou a ver apenas aos 76 anos, em 1995. Nessa época, já era uma das melhores escritoras de língua inglesa revelada no continente africano.

Continuou escrevendo após abandonar a família, mas não publicou nada até sete anos terem se passado. Seu primeiro romance foi *The Grass is Singing* [A grama está cantando]. Tinha 31 anos. Fazia um ano que tinha se instalado em Londres e seis que tinha voltado a se casar, dessa vez com Gottfried Lessing, de quem adotou o sobrenome. Gottfried era judeu e comunista, havia nascido em São Petersburgo e fugido da Alemanha quando Hitler chegou ao poder. Conheceu Doris no Zimbábue. Não demorariam a se separar, porém antes teriam um filho, com quem a autora se mudou para Londres em 1949.

A *The Grass is Singing* seguiriam as histórias de *This was the Old Chief's Country* [Este era o país do velho chefe], em 1951, e praticamente um romance por ano (ou uma recopilação de contos e até mesmo um livro de poemas) até a edição de *The Golden Notebook* [O Caderno Dourado], em 1962, para muitos (na realidade, muitas) sua obra-prima. Pedra angular do feminismo dos anos 1960, narra as peripécias de Anna Wulf, escritora, *alter ego* da autora, ao longo de cerca de uma década. Construído em forma de diário, o romance é um discurso a favor da liberdade da mulher, frustrado pela realidade asfixiante dos anos 1950, quando ser mulher não era nada fácil. Mas não é só isso. No *The Golden Notebook*, Lessing saldava suas contas com o comunismo, que acabou se tornando uma das maiores decepções de sua vida.

Sua obra, extensa e das mais variadas (quase meia centena de livros), seguiu tocando na ferida (o comunismo, mas também a falsa liberdade da mulher e a sua infância e adolescência na África) e transformou Lessing no epicentro de um terremoto literário e social diante do qual a Academia Sueca acabou se rendendo em 2007, quando lhe foi concedido o Nobel de Literatura.

LAURA FERNÁNDEZ

APRESENTAÇÃO DO CONTO
To Room Nineteen

Todo mundo sonha em ter vizinhos como os Rawlings e ter, como eles, uma casa extraordinária (enorme, branca e com muita grama para cortar), quatro filhos (agitados, claro, mas não são todos assim?), um destino diferente todas as férias, trabalhos invejáveis e um sorriso sempre a postos. De forma que, sim, todo mundo queria ser Susan Rawlings. Todos, menos ela. No entanto, e isso é curioso, Susan nem sequer o sabe.

 Quando começa este conto, um dos mais autobiográficos e brutais de Doris Lessing, Susan é uma dona de casa atarefada: teve de deixar o trabalho quando nasceram os gêmeos e precisa dar conta de quatro filhos e de uma mansão de três andares. As crianças começam a ir ao colégio, ela recupera parte do seu tempo e, sem se dar conta, se desdobra em novas funções.

Pouco a pouco, começa a abandonar a casa e a se transportar para outro lugar mental, onde não é mais uma mãe de família, e sim uma solteira solitária que passa as tardes em um quarto de hotel.

Publicado originalmente como parte da antologia *A Man and Two Women* [Um homem e duas mulheres], editada em 1963, "To Room Nineteen" é um dos melhores exemplos da luta literária da autora, que ganharia o Nobel em 2007 por "sua capacidade de transmitir a característica épica da experiência feminina". Doris Lessing expressa neste conto sua própria experiência. Casou-se duas vezes e duas vezes se divorciou. Do primeiro casamento, deixou para trás seus dois filhos, que só voltou a ver aos 76 anos. A situação dramática na qual Susan se encontra, essa luta interna entre o amor que sente por seus filhos e seu marido e o seu desejo de ser livre — mesmo que a liberdade signifique pouco mais do que uma poltrona junto à janela em um cubículo — é algo que Lessing conhecia bem. Foi o que quis explorar por meio desse tipo de sonho familiar truncado que sugerem os Rawlings, uma brutal descida aos infernos do perfeito cortador de grama perto da piscina, do cartão-postal amassado que uma mulher envia a seu eu perdido.

Formalmente, a história está tão ordenada quanto o estaria a mansão dos Rawlings em um domingo de visita. Tudo começa com um vislumbre de um fantasma cruzando o quarto, que representa a plácida vida familiar; o fantasma vai construindo seu pequeno reino pouco a pouco, conforme a trama avança, sempre de forma precisa e com uma simplicidade avassaladora.

Afiadas como facas, as conversas de Susan com seu marido se sucedem como cataclismos inevitáveis, em um ir e vir de roupas sem passar, crianças, barulho e uma infinidade de detalhes cotidianos. Estes constituem o grosso do vocabulário que aprenderemos graças a este conto e ao glossário, que esclarece nuances e significados em cada uma das páginas. A sonoridade dos corações partidos que palpitam em "To Room Nineteen" também pode ser desfrutada na emocionante versão incluída no CD. Entenda-se emocionante no sentido de "abalar corações", mas também de sacudida brutal em um mundo que lamentavelmente não tem por que ser como o pintam.

LAURA FERNÁNDEZ

To Room Nineteen

This is a story, I suppose, about a failure in intelligence[1]: the Rawlingses' marriage was grounded[2] in intelligence.

They were older when they married than most of their married friends: in their well-seasoned late twenties[3]. Both had had a number of affairs[4], sweet rather than bitter[5]; and when they fell in love – for they did fall in love – had known each other for some time. They joked that they had saved each other[6] 'for the real thing'. That they had waited so long (but not too long) for this real thing was to them a proof of their sensible discrimination[7]. A good many of their friends had married young, and now (they felt) probably regretted lost opportunities; while others, still unmarried, seemed to them arid, self-doubting[8], and likely to[9] make desperate or romantic marriages.

Not only they, but others, felt they were well-matched[10]: their friends' delight[11] was an additional proof of their happiness. They had played the same roles, male and female, in this group or set, if such a wide, loosely connected[12], constantly changing constellation of people could be called a set[13]. They had both become, by virtue of their moderation, their humour,

---

1 **a failure in intelligence:** fracasso da inteligência • 2 **grounded:** baseado • 3 **well-seasoned late twenties:** vinte e tantos anos bem vividos • 4 **a number of affairs:** uma série de casos • 5 **bitter:** amargos • 6 **they had saved each other:** tinham se guardado um para o outro • 7 **sensible discrimination:** um discernimento sensato • 8 **self-doubting:** hesitantes • 9 **likely to:** propensos a • 10 **they were well-matched:** eles combinavam bem • 11 **delight:** prazer • 12 **loosely connected:** conectados livremente • 13 **a set:** um grupo

and their abstinence from painful experience, people to whom others came for advice. They could be, and were, relied on[1]. It was one of those cases of a man and a woman linking themselves whom no one else had ever thought of linking, probably because of their similarities. But then everyone exclaimed: Of course! How right! How was it we never thought of it before!

And so they married amid general rejoicing[2], and because of their foresight[3] and their sense for what was probable, nothing was a surprise to them.

Both had well-paid jobs. Matthew was a sub-editor[4] on a large London newspaper, and Susan worked in an advertising firm. He was not the stuff[5] of which editors or publicised journalists[6] are made, but he was much more than 'a sub-editor', being one of the essential background people[7] who in fact steady[8], inspire and make possible the people in the limelight[9]. He was content[10] with this position. Susan had a talent for commercial drawing[11]. She was humorous about the advertisements she was responsible for, but she did not feel strongly about them[12] one way or the other.

Both, before they married, had had pleasant flats, but they felt it unwise[13] to base a marriage on either flat, because it might seem like a submission of personality on the part of the one whose flat it was not. They moved into a new flat in South Kensington[14] on the clear understanding that when their mar-

---

1 **they could be, and were, relied on:** podiam ser e eram confiáveis • 2 **amid general rejoicing:** em meio a uma alegria geral • 3 **foresight:** previsão • 4 **sub-editor:** subeditor • 5 **he was not the stuff:** ele não era feito do material • 6 **publicised journalists:** jornalistas de renome • 7 **essential background people:** pessoas essenciais dos bastidores • 8 **steady:** dão estabilidade • 9 **the people in the limelight:** as pessoas no centro das atenções • 10 **content:** satisfeito • 11 **commercial drawing:** ilustração publicitária • 12 **she did not feel strongly about them:** não vibrava muito com eles • 13 **unwise:** pouco sábio • 14 **South Kensington:** bairro confortável de Londres

riage had settled down (a process they knew would not take long, and was in fact more a humorous concession to popular wisdom[1] than what was due to themselves) they would buy a house and start a family.

And this is what happened. They lived in their charming flat[2] for two years, giving parties and going to them, being a popular young married couple, and then Susan became pregnant, she gave up her job, and they bought a house in Richmond[3]. It was typical of this couple[4] that they had a son first, then a daughter, then twins, son and daughter. Everything right, appropriate, and what everyone would wish for, if they could choose. But people did feel these two had chosen; this balanced and sensible family was no more than what was due to them because of their infallible sense for *choosing* right.

And so they lived with their four children in their gardened house[5] in Richmond and were happy. They had everything they had wanted and had planned for.

And yet . . .

Well, even this was expected, that there must be a certain flatness[6] . . .

Yes, yes, of course, it was natural they sometimes felt like this. Like what?

Their life seemed to be like a snake biting its tail. Matthew's job for the sake of Susan, children, house, and garden[7] – which caravanserai[8] needed a well-paid job to maintain it. And Susan's practical intelligence for the sake of Matthew, the children, the

---

1 **popular wisdom:** sabedoria popular • 2 **charming flat:** apartamento encantador • 3 **Richmond:** distrito próximo a Londres • 4 **it was typical of this couple:** era típico desse casal • 5 **gardened house:** casa com jardim • 6 **flatness:** monotonia • 7 **Matthew's job for the sake of Susan, children, house and garden:** o trabalho de Matthew para sustentar Susan, as crianças, a casa e o jardim • 8 **which caravanserai:** que parecia um hotel (na realidade, caravançará, pousadas no deserto do Oriente para as grandes caravanas)

house and the garden – which unit¹ would have collapsed in a week without her.

But there was no point about which either could say: 'For the sake *of this* is all the rest.' Children? But children can't be a centre of life and a reason for being. They can be a thousand things that are delightful, interesting, satisfying, but they can't be a wellspring² to live from. Or they shouldn't be. Susan and Matthew knew that well enough.

Matthew's job? Ridiculous. It was an interesting job, but scarcely³ a reason for living. Matthew took pride⁴ in doing it well, but he could hardly be expected to be proud of the newspaper; the newspaper he read, *his* newspaper, was not the one he worked for.

Their love for each other? Well, that was nearest it⁵. If this wasn't a centre, what was? Yes, it was around this point, their love, that the whole extraordinary structure revolved⁶. For extraordinary it certainly was⁷. Both Susan and Matthew had moments of thinking so, of looking in secret disbelief⁸ at this thing they had created: marriage, four children, big house, garden, charwomen⁹, friends, cars . . . and this *thing*, this entity, all of it had come into existence, been blown into being out of nowhere¹⁰, because Susan loved Matthew and Matthew loved Susan. Extraordinary. So that was the central point, the wellspring.

And if one felt that it simply was not strong enough, important enough, to support it all¹¹, well whose fault was that? Certainly

---

1 **which unit:** cuja unidade • 2 **wellspring:** fonte • 3 **scarcely:** dificilmente • 4 **took pride:** tinha orgulho • 5 **nearest it:** o que mais se aproximava de • 6 **revolved:** girava • 7 **for extraordinary it certainly was:** porque era certamente extraordinária • 8 **secret disbelief:** ceticismo interno • 9 **charwomen:** criadas • 10 **(had) been blown into being out of nowhere:** havia surgido do nada • 11 **to support it all:** para sustentar tudo isso

neither Susan's nor Matthew's. It was in the nature of things. And they sensibly blamed neither themselves nor each other.

On the contrary, they used their intelligence to preserve[1] what they had created from a painful and explosive world: they looked around them, and took lessons. All around them, marriages collapsing, or breaking, or rubbing along[2] (even worse, they felt). They must not make the same mistakes, they must not.

They had avoided the pitfall[3] so many of their friends had fallen into – of buying a house in the country *for the sake of the children*, so that the husband became a weekend husband, a weekend father, and the wife always careful not to ask what went on in the town flat which they called (in joke) a bachelor flat[4]. No, Matthew was a full-time husband, a full-time father, and at night, in the big married bed in the big married bedroom (which had an attractive view of the river), they lay beside each other talking and he told her about his day, and what he had done, and whom he had met; and she told him about her day (not as interesting, but that was not her fault), for both knew of the hidden resentments and deprivations[5] of the woman who has lived her own life – and above all, has earned her own living – and is now dependent on a husband for outside interests[6] and money.

Nor did Susan make the mistake of taking a job for the sake of her independence, which she might very well have done, since her old firm, missing her qualities of humour, balance[7], and sense[8], invited her often to go back. Children needed their

1 **to preserve:** conservar • 2 **rubbing along:** sendo levados com a barriga • 3 **pitfall:** armadilha • 4 **a bachelor flat:** um apartamento de solteiro • 5 **hidden resentments and deprivations:** os ressentimentos e privações ocultos • 6 **outside interests:** tudo que se refere ao mundo externo • 7 **balance:** equilíbrio • 8 **sense:** bom senso

mother to a certain age, that both parents knew and agreed on; and when these four healthy wisely brought up children[1] were of the right age, Susan would work again, because she knew, and so did he, what happened to women of fifty at the height[2] of their energy and ability, with grown-up children who no longer needed their full devotion.

So here was this couple, testing their marriage, looking after it[3], treating it like a small boat full of helpless people in a very stormy sea. Well, of course, so it was... The storms of the world were bad, but not too close – which is not to say they were selfishly felt[4]: Susan and Matthew were both well-informed and responsible people. And the inner storms and quicksands[5] were understood and charted[6]. So everything was all right. Everything was in order. Yes, things were under control.

So what did it matter if they felt dry[7], flat[8]? People like themselves, fed on[9] a hundred books (psychological, anthropological, sociological), could scarcely be unprepared[10] for the dry, controlled wistfulness[11] which is the distinguishing mark of the intelligent marriage. Two people, endowed with[12] education, with discrimination[13], with judgement, linked together[14] voluntarily from their will to be happy together and to be of use to others – one sees them everywhere, one knows them, one even is that thing oneself: sadness because so much is after all so little[15]. These two, unsurprised, turned towards each other

---

1 **healthy wisely brought up children:** crianças sadias e bem-criadas • 2 **at the height:** no apogeu • 3 **looking after it:** cuidando dele • 4 **which is not to say they were selfishly felt:** o que não quer dizer que fossem egoístas • 5 **inner storms and quicksands:** e as tormentas e areias movediças internas • 6 **charted:** mapeadas • 7 **dry:** murchos • 8 **flat:** monótonos • 9 **fed on:** se alimentavam de • 10 **could scarcely be unprepared:** dificilmente poderiam estar despreparadas • 11 **wistfulness:** nostalgia • 12 **endowed with:** dotadas de • 13 **discrimination:** bom senso • 14 **linked together:** unidas • 15 **so much is after all so little:** tanto é, afinal, tão pouco

with even more courtesy and gentle love: this was life, that two people, no matter how carefully chosen, could not be everything to each other. In fact, even to say so, to think in such a way, was banal; they were ashamed to do it.

It was banal, too, when one night Matthew came home late and confessed he had been to a party, taken a girl home and slept with her. Susan forgave him, of course. Except that forgiveness is hardly the word. Understanding, yes. But if you understand something, you don't forgive it, you are the thing itself: forgiveness is for what you *don't* understand. Nor had he *confessed* – what sort of word is that?

The whole thing was not important. After all, years ago they had joked: Of course I'm not going to be faithful[1] to you, no one can be faithful to one other person for a whole lifetime. (And there was the word 'faithful' – stupid, all these words, stupid, belonging to a savage old world[2].) But the incident left both of them irritable. Strange, but they were both bad-tempered[3], annoyed[4]. There was something unassimilable about it.

Making love splendidly after he had come home that night, both had felt that the idea that Myra Jenkins, a pretty girl met at a party, could be even relevant was ridiculous. They had loved each other for over a decade, would love each other for years more[5]. Who, then, was Myra Jenkins?

Except, thought Susan, unaccountably bad-tempered[6], she was (is?) the first. In ten years. So either the ten years' fidelity was not important, or she isn't. (No, no, there is something wrong with this way of thinking, there must be.) But if she isn't important, presumably it wasn't important either when

---

1 **faithful:** fiel • 2 **a savage old world:** um mundo velho e bárbaro • 3 **bad-tempered:** mal-humorados • 4 **annoyed:** incomodados • 5 **for years more:** muitos anos mais • 6 **unaccountably bad-tempered:** inexplicavelmente mal--humorada

Matthew and I first went to bed with each other that afternoon whose delight even now (like a very long shadow at sundown[1]) lays a long, wand-like finger[2] over us. (Why did I say sundown?) Well, if what we felt that afternoon was not important, nothing is important, because if it hadn't been for what we felt, we wouldn't be Mr and Mrs Rawlings with four children, et cetera, et cetera. The whole thing is *absurd* – for him to have come home and told me was absurd. For him not to have told me was absurd. For me to care or, for that matter[3], not to care, is absurd . . . and who is Myra Jenkins? Why[4], no one at all.

There was only one thing to do, and of course these sensible people did it; they put the thing behind them, and consciously, knowing what they were doing, moved forward into a different phase of their marriage, giving thanks for past good fortune as they did so.

For it was inevitable that the handsome, blonde, attractive, manly[5] man, Matthew Rawlings, should be at times tempted (oh, what a word!) by the attractive girls at parties she could not attend[6] because of the four children; and that sometimes he would succumb (a word even more repulsive, if possible) and that she, a good-looking woman in the big well-tended garden[7] at Richmond, would sometimes be pierced as by an arrow[8] from the sky with bitterness. Except that bitterness was not in order, it was out of court[9]. Did the casual girls[10] touch the marriage? They did not. Rather it was they who knew defeat because of the handsome Matthew Rawlings' marriage body and soul to Susan Rawlings.

---

1 **sundown:** entardecer • 2 **wand-like finger:** um dedo mágico • 3 **for that matter:** na verdade • 4 **why:** ora! • 5 **manly:** viril • 6 **attend:** comparecer • 7 **well-tended garden:** jardim bem cuidado • 8 **pierced as by an arrow:** atravessada como por uma flecha • 9 **was not in order, it was out of court:** não era apropriada, não era admissível • 10 **the casual girls:** eventuais casos

In that case why did Susan feel (though luckily not for longer than a *few* seconds at a time) as if life had become a desert, and that nothing mattered, and that her children were not her own?

Meanwhile her intelligence continued to assert[1] that all was well. What if her Matthew did have an occasional sweet afternoon, the odd affair[2]? For she knew quite well, except in her moments of aridity[3], that they were very happy, that the affairs were not important.

Perhaps that was the trouble? It was in the nature of things that the adventures and delights could no longer be hers, because of the four children and the big house that needed so much attention. But perhaps she was secretly wishing, and even knowing that she did, that the wildness[4] and the beauty could be his. But he was married to her. She was married to him. They were married inextricably. And therefore the gods could not strike him[5] with the real magic, not really. Well, was it Susan's fault that after he came home from an adventure he looked harassed[6] rather than fulfilled[7]? (In fact, that was how she knew he had been *unfaithful*, because of his sullen air[8], and his glances[9] at her, similar to hers at him: What is it that I share with this person that shields all delight from me[10]?) But none of it by anybody's fault. (But what did they feel ought to be somebody's fault?) Nobody's fault, nothing to be at fault, no one to blame[11], no one to offer or to take it . . . and nothing wrong, either, except that Matthew never was really struck, as

---

1 **to assert:** afirmar • 2 **the odd affair:** algum caso ocasional • 3 **moments of aridity:** momentos de aridez • 4 **wildness:** ímpeto • 5 **could not strike him:** não podiam atingi-lo • 6 **harassed:** atormentado • 7 **fullfilled:** satisfeito • 8 **sullen air:** ar taciturno • 9 **glances:** olhares • 10 **that shields all delight from me:** que me impede de sentir prazer • 11 **to blame:** culpar

he wanted to be, by joy[1]; and that Susan was more and more often threatened by emptiness. (It was usually in the garden that she was invaded by this feeling: she was coming to avoid[2] the garden, unless the children or Matthew were with her.) There was no need to use the dramatic words 'unfaithful', 'forgive', and the rest: intelligence forbade them[3]. Intelligence barred[4], too, quarrelling[5], sulking[6], anger, silences of withdrawal[7], accusations and tears. Above all, intelligence forbids tears.

A high price has to be paid for the happy marriage with the four healthy children in the large white gardened house.

And they were paying it, willingly[8], knowing what they were doing. When they lay side by side or breast to breast in the big civilised bedroom overlooking the wild sullied[9] river, they laughed, often, for no particular reason; but they knew it was really because of these two small people, Susan and Matthew, supporting such an edifice on their intelligent love. The laugh comforted them; it saved them both, though from what, they did not know.

They were now both fortyish[10]. The older children, boy and girl, were ten and eight, at school. The twins, six, were still at home. Susan did not have nurses or girls to help her: childhood is short; and she did not regret[11] the hard work. Often enough[12] she was bored, since small children can be boring; she was often very tired; but she regretted nothing. In another decade, she would turn herself back into being a woman with a life of her own.

1 **never was really struck, as he wanted to be, by joy:** nunca se sentiu, como queria, plenamente feliz • 2 **she was coming to avoid:** ela chegava a evitar • 3 **forbade them:** os proibia • 4 **barred:** impedia • 5 **quarrelling:** discussões • 6 **sulking:** mau humor • 7 **silences of withdrawal:** silêncios de isolamento • 8 **willingly:** de bom grado • 9 **wild sullied:** poluído e selvagem • 10 **fortyish:** quarentões • 11 **she did not regret:** ela não se arrependia • 12 **often enough:** com bastante frequência

Soon the twins would go to school, and they would be away from home from nine until four. These hours, so Susan saw it, would be the preparation for her own slow emancipation away from the role of hub-of-the-family[1] into woman-with-her-own-life. She was already planning for the hours of freedom when all the children would be 'off her hands[2]'. That was the phrase used by Matthew and by Susan and by their friends, for the moment when the youngest child went off to school. 'They'll be off your hands, darling Susan, and you'll have time to yourself.' So said Matthew, the intelligent husband, who had often enough commended[3] and consoled Susan, standing by her[4] in spirit during the years when her soul was not her own, as she said, but her children's.

What it amounted to[5] was that Susan saw herself as she had been at twenty-eight, unmarried; and then again somewhere about fifty, blossoming from the root[6] of what she had been twenty years before. As if the essential Susan were in abeyance[7], as if she were in cold storage[8]. Matthew said something like this to Susan one night: and she agreed that it was true – she did feel something like that. What, then, was this essential Susan? She did not know. Put like that it sounded ridiculous, and she did not really feel it. Anyway, they had a long discussion[9] about the whole thing before going off to sleep[10] in each other's arms.

So the twins went off to their school, two bright affectionate[11] children who had no problems about it, since their older

---

1 **the role of hub-of-the family:** o papel de pilar da família • 2 **off her hands:** fora de seus cuidados • 3 **commended:** elogiado • 4 **standing by her:** apoiando-a • 5 **what it amounted to:** o caso é que • 6 **blossoming from the root:** renascendo das raízes • 7 **in abeyance:** em suspenso • 8 **in cold storage:** congelada • 9 **discussion:** conversa • 10 **going off to sleep:** antes de dormir • 11 **affectionate:** carinhosas

brother and sister had trodden this path so successfully[1] before them. And now Susan was going to be alone in the big house, every day of the school term[2], except for the daily woman who came in to clean.

It was now, for the first time in this marriage, that something happened which neither of them had foreseen[3].

This is what happened. She returned, at nine-thirty, from taking the twins to the school by car, looking forward to seven blissful[4] hours of freedom. On the first morning she was simply restless[5], worrying about the twins, 'naturally enough' since this was their first day away at school. She was hardly able to contain herself until they came back. Which they did happily, excited by the world of school, looking forward to[6] the next day. And the next day Susan took them, dropped them[7], came back, and found herself reluctant[8] to enter her big and beautiful home because it was as if something was waiting for her there that she did not wish to confront[9]. Sensibly[10], however, she parked the car in the garage, entered the house, spoke to Mrs Parkes, the daily woman, about her duties[11], and went up to her bedroom. She was possessed by a fever which drove her out[12] again, downstairs, into the kitchen, where Mrs Parkes was making cake and did not need her, and into the garden. There she sat on a bench and tried to calm herself looking at trees, at a brown glimpse[13] of the river. But she was filled with tension, like a panic: as if an enemy was in the garden with her. She spoke to herself severely, thus: All this is quite

---

1 **had trodden this path so successfully:** haviam trilhado esse caminho com tanto êxito • 2 **school term:** período escolar • 3 **had foreseen:** tinha previsto • 4 **blissful:** abençoadas • 5 **restless:** inquieta • 6 **looking forward to:** esperando ansiosamente • 7 **dropped them:** deixou-os • 8 **reluctant:** relutante • 9 **confront:** encarar • 10 **sensibly:** com sensatez • 11 **duties:** tarefas •12 **drove her out:** a conduziu para fora • 13 **glimpse:** vislumbre

natural. First, I spent twelve years of my adult life working, *living my own life*. Then I married, and from the moment I became pregnant for the first time I signed myself over, so to speak, to other people[1]. To the children. Not for one moment in twelve years have I been alone, had time to myself. So now I have to learn to be myself again. That's all.

And she went indoors to help Mrs Parkes cook and clean, and found some sewing[2] to do for the children. She kept herself occupied every day. At the end of the first term she understood she felt two contrary emotions. First: secret astonishment and dismay[3] that during those weeks when the house was empty of children she had in fact been more occupied (had been careful to keep herself occupied) than ever she had been when the children were around her needing her continual attention. Second: that now she knew the house would be full of them, and for five weeks, she resented[4] the fact she would never be alone. She was already looking back at those hours of sewing, cooking (but by herself[5]) as at a lost freedom which would not be hers for five long weeks. And the two months of term which would succeed the five weeks stretched alluringly open to her – freedom[6]. But what freedom – when in fact she had been so careful not to be free of small duties during the last weeks? She looked at herself, Susan Rawlings, sitting in a big chair by the window in the bedroom, sewing shirts or dresses, which she might just as well have bought. She saw herself making cakes for hours at a time[7] in the big family kitchen: yet usually she bought cakes. What she saw was a woman alone, that was true,

1 **I signed myself over, so to speak, to other people:** eu renunciei a mim mesma, por assim dizer, em favor de outras pessoas • 2 **sewing:** costura • 3 **astonishment and dismay:** assombro e desânimo • 4 **she resented:** ela lamentou • 5 **but by herself:** mas sozinha • 6 **stretched alluringly open to her – freedom:** se estendiam de forma tentadora para sua... liberdade • 7 **for hours at a time:** muitas horas seguidas

but she had not felt alone. For instance, Mrs Parkes was always somewhere in the house. And she did not like being in the garden at all, because of the closeness there of the enemy – irritation, restlessness, emptiness, whatever it was – which keeping her hands occupied made less dangerous for some reason.

Susan did not tell Matthew of these thoughts. They were not sensible[1]. She did not recognise herself in them. What should she say to her dear friend and husband, Matthew? 'When I go into the garden, that is[2], if the children are not there, I feel as if there is an enemy there waiting to invade me.' 'What enemy, Susan darling?' 'Well I don't know, really ... ' 'Perhaps you should see a doctor?'

No, clearly this conversation should not take place. The holidays began and Susan welcomed them. Four children, lively, energetic, intelligent, demanding[3]: she was never, not for a moment of her day, alone. If she was in a room, they would be in the next room, or waiting for her to do something for them; or it would soon be time for lunch or tea[4], or to take one of them to the dentist. Something to do: five weeks of it, thank goodness.

On the fourth day of these so welcome holidays, she found she was storming with anger[5] at the twins; two shrinking[6] beautiful children who (and this is what checked her[7]) stood hand in hand looking at her with sheer dismayed disbelief[8]. This was their calm mother, shouting at them. And for what? They had come to her with some game, some bit of nonsense. They looked at each other, moved closer for support, and went off[9] hand in hand, leaving Susan holding on to the windowsill[10]

---

1 **sensible:** sensatos • 2 **that is:** isto é • 3 **demanding:** exigentes • 4 **tea:** chá da tarde • 5 **storming with anger:** berrando com raiva • 6 **shrinking:** se encolhiam • 7 **checked her:** a freou • 8 **sheer dismayed disbelief:** real e assustada incredulidade • 9 **went off:** e foram embora • 10 **holding on to the windowsill:** segurando no peitoril da janela

of the living-room, breathing deep, feeling sick. She went to lie down, telling the older children she had a headache. She heard the boy Harry telling the little ones: 'It's all right, Mother's got a headache.' She heard that *It's all right* with pain.

That night she said to her husband: 'Today I shouted at the twins, quite unfairly.' She sounded miserable[1], and he said gently: 'Well, what of it[2]?'

'It's more of an adjustment than I thought[3], their going to school.'

'But Susie, Susie darling . . .' For she was crouched weeping on the bed[4]. He comforted her: 'Susan, what is all this about? You shouted at them? What of it? If you shouted at them fifty times a day it wouldn't be more than the little devils deserve[5].' But she wouldn't laugh. She wept. Soon he comforted her with his body. She became calm. Calm, she wondered what was wrong with her, and why she should mind so much that she might, just once, have behaved unjustly with the children. What did it matter? They had forgotten it all long ago: Mother had a headache and everything was all right.

It was a long time later that Susan understood that that night, when she had wept and Matthew had driven the misery out of her with his big solid body, was the last time, ever in their married life, that they had been – to use their mutual language – with each other. And even that was a lie, because she had not told him of her real fears at all.

The five weeks passed, and Susan was in control of herself, and good and kind, and she looked forward to the holidays with a mixture of fear and longing[6]. She did not know what

---

1 **miserable:** chateada • 2 **well, what of it?:** bom, e daí? • 3 **it's more of an adjustment than I thought:** está sendo mais difícil me acostumar do que eu imaginava • 4 **she was crouched weeping on the bed:** ela estava encolhida chorando na cama • 5 **deserve:** merecem • 6 **longing:** saudade

to expect. She took the twins off to school (the elder children took themselves to school) and she returned to the house determined to face the enemy wherever he was, in the house, or the garden or – where?

She was again restless, she was possessed by restlessness. She cooked and sewed and worked as before, day after day, while Mrs Parkes remonstrated[1]: 'Mrs Rawlings, what's the need for it? I can do that, it's what you pay me for.'

And it was so irrational that she checked herself[2]. She would put the car into the garage, go up to her bedroom, and sit, hands in her lap, forcing herself to be quiet. She listened to Mrs Parkes moving around the house. She looked out into the garden and saw the branches shake[3] the trees. She sat defeating[4] the enemy, restlessness. Emptiness. She ought to be thinking about her life, about herself. But she did not. Or perhaps she could not. As soon as she forced her mind to think about Susan (for what else did she want to be alone for?), it skipped off to[5] thoughts of butter or school clothes. Or it thought of Mrs Parkes. She realised that she sat listening for the movements of the cleaning woman, following her every turn, bend[6], thought. She followed her in her mind from kitchen to bathroom, from table to oven[7], and it was as if the duster[8], the cleaning cloth, the saucepan[9], were in her own hand. She would hear herself saying: No, not like that, don't put that there . . . Yet she did not give a damn[10] what Mrs Parkes did, or if she did it at all. Yet she could not prevent herself[11] from being conscious of her, every minute. Yes, this was what was wrong with her: she needed, when she was alone, to be really alone, with no one near. She

---

1 **remonstrated:** protestava • 2 **she checked herself:** ela se continha • 3 **shake:** agitando • 4 **defeating:** vencendo • 5 **it skipped off to:** desviava para • 6 **bend:** volta • 7 **oven:** forno • 8 **duster:** espanador • 9 **saucepan:** panela • 10 **she did not give a damn:** ela não dava a mínima • 11 **prevent herself:** evitar

could not endure the knowledge¹ that in ten minutes or in half an hour Mrs Parkes would call up the stairs²: 'Mrs Rawlings, there's no silver polish³. Madam, we're out of flour⁴.'

So she left the house and went to sit in the garden where she was screened⁵ from the house by trees. She waited for the demon⁶ to appear and claim her⁷, but he did not.

She was keeping him off⁸, because she had not, after all, come to an end of arranging herself⁹.

She was planning how to be somewhere where Mrs Parkes would not come after her with a cup of tea, or a demand¹⁰ to be allowed to telephone (always irritating, since¹¹ Susan did not care who she telephoned or how often), or just a nice talk about something. Yes, she needed a place, or a state of affairs, where it would not be necessary to keep reminding herself: In ten minutes I must telephone Matthew about . . . and at half-past three I must leave early for the children because the car needs cleaning. And at ten o'clock tomorrow I must remember . . . She was possessed with resentment that the seven hours of freedom in every day (during weekdays¹² in the school term) were not free, that never, not for one second, ever, was she free from the pressure of time, from having to remember this or that. She could never forget herself; never really let herself go into forgetfulness¹³.

Resentment. It was poisoning¹⁴ her. (She looked at this emotion and thought it was absurd. Yet she felt it.) She was a

---

1 **she could not endure the knowledge:** ela não podia suportar saber • 2 **would call up the stairs:** gritaria na escada • 3 **silver polish:** produto para polir prata • 4 **we're out of flour:** estamos sem farinha • 5 **screened:** oculta; coberta • 6 **demon:** demônio • 7 **claim her:** reivindicá-la • 8 **she was keeping him off:** o mantinha afastado • 9 **she had not ... come to an end of arranging herself:** por que não havia chegado a se organizar • 10 **demand:** pedido • 11 **since:** já que • 12 **weekdays:** dias úteis • 13 **never really let herself go into forgetfulness:** nunca se permitia uma só distração • 14 **poisoning:** envenenando

prisoner. (She looked at this thought too, and it was no good telling herself it was a ridiculous one.) She must tell Matthew – but what? She was filled with emotions that were utterly[1] ridiculous, that she despised[2], yet that nevertheless she was feeling so strongly she could not shake them off[3].

The school holidays came round, and this time they were for nearly two months, and she behaved with a conscious controlled decency[4] that nearly drove her crazy. She would lock herself[5] in the bathroom, and sit on the edge[6] of the bath, breathing deep, trying to let go into some kind of calm. Or she went up into the spare room[7], usually empty, where no one would expect her to be. She heard the children calling 'Mother, Mother,' and kept silent, feeling guilty. Or she went to the very end of the garden, by herself, and looked at the slow-moving brown river; she looked at the river and closed her eyes and breathed slow and deep, taking it into her being[8], into her veins.

Then she returned to the family, wife and mother, smiling and responsible, feeling as if the pressure of these people – four lively children and her husband – were a painful pressure on the surface of her skin, a hand pressing on her brain. She did not once break down into irritation[9] during these holidays, but it was like living out a prison sentence, and when the children went back to school, she sat on a white stone near the flowing river, and she thought: It is not even a year since the twins went to school, since *they were off my hands* (What on earth[10] did I think I meant when I used that stupid phrase?), and yet I'm a different person. I'm simply not myself. I don't understand it.

1 **utterly:** totalmente • 2 **she despised:** ela desprezava • 3 **shake them off:** se livrar delas • 4 **decency:** decência • 5 **she would lock herself:** se trancava no banheiro • 6 **edge:** borda • 7 **spare room:** quarto de hóspedes vazio • 8 **taking it into her being:** aspirando o ar para dentro do seu ser • 9 **she did not once break down into irritation:** ela em nenhum momento explodiu de irritação • 10 **what on earth:** que diabos

Yet she had to understand it. For she knew that this structure – big white house, on which the mortgage[1] still cost four hundred a year, a husband, so good and kind and insightful[2]; four children, all doing so nicely; and the garden where she sat; and Mrs Parkes, the cleaning woman – all this depended on her, and yet she could not understand why, or even what it was she contributed to it.

She said to Matthew in their bedroom: 'I think there must be something wrong with me.'

And he said: 'Surely not, Susan? You look marvellous – you're as lovely as ever.'

She looked at the handsome blonde man, with his clear[3], intelligent, blue-eyed face, and thought: Why is it I can't tell him? Why not? And she said: 'I need to be alone more than I am.'

At which he swung his slow blue gaze at her[4], and she saw what she had been dreading[5]: incredulity. Disbelief. And fear. An incredulous blue stare from a stranger who was her husband, as close to her as her own breath.

He said: 'But the children are at school and off your hands.'

She said to herself: I've got to force myself to say: Yes, but do you realise that I never feel free? There's never a moment I can say to myself: There's nothing I have to remind myself about, nothing I have to do in half an hour, or an hour, or two hours . . .

But she said: 'I don't feel well.'

He said: 'Perhaps you need a holiday.'

She said, appalled[6]: 'But not without you, surely?' For she could not imagine herself going off without him. Yet that was

---

1 **mortgage:** hipoteca • 2 **insightful:** perspicaz • 3 **clear:** claro • 4 **at which he swung his slow blue gaze at her:** ele respondeu desviando lentamente o olhar azul em sua direção • 5 **what she had been dreading:** o que temia • 6 **appalled:** consternada

what he meant. Seeing her face, he laughed, and opened his arms, and she went into them, thinking: Yes, yes, but why can't I say it? And what is it I have to say?

She tried to tell him, about never being free. And he listened and said: 'But Susan, what sort of freedom can you possibly want – short of being dead[1]! Am I ever free? I go to the office, and I have to be there at ten – all right, half-past ten, sometimes. And I have to do this or that, don't I? Then I've got to come home at a certain time – I don't mean it, you know I don't[2] – but if I'm not going to be back home at six I telephone you. When can I ever say to myself: I have nothing to be responsible for in the next six hours?'

Susan, hearing this, was remorseful[3]. Because it was true. The good marriage, the house, the children, depended just as much on his voluntary bondage[4] as it did on hers. But why did he not feel bound? Why didn't he chafe[5] and become restless? No, there was something really wrong with her and this proved it.

And that word 'bondage' – why had she used it? She had never felt marriage, or the children, as bondage. Neither had he, or surely they wouldn't be together lying in each other's arms content after twelve years of marriage.

No, her state (whatever it was) was irrelevant, nothing to do with her real good life with her family. She had to accept the fact: that, after all, she was an irrational person and to live with it. Some people had to live with crippled arms[6], or stammers[7], or being deaf. She would have to live knowing she was subject to a state of mind she could not own.

---

1 **short of being dead!:** a menos que seja a morte • 2 **I don't mean it, you know I don't:** não me importo, você sabe que não • 3 **remorseful:** arrependida • 4 **bondage:** sujeição • 5 **he chafe:** irritava • 6 **crippled arms:** braços aleijados • 7 **stammers:** gagueira

Nevertheless, as a result of this conversation with her husband, there was a new regime next holidays.

The spare room at the top of the house now had a cardboard sign saying: PRIVATE! DO NOT DISTURB! on it. (This sign had been drawn in coloured chalks[1] by the children, after a discussion between the parents in which it was decided this was psychologically the right thing.) The family and Mrs Parkes knew this was 'Mother's Room' and that she was entitled to[2] her privacy. Many serious conversations took place between Matthew and the children about not taking Mother for granted[3]. Susan overheard[4] the first, between father and Harry, the older boy, and was surprised at her irritation over it. Surely she could have a room somewhere in that big house and retire into it without such a fuss[5] being made? Without it being so solemnly discussed? Why couldn't she simply have announced: 'I'm going to fit out[6] the little top room for myself, and when I'm in it I'm not to be disturbed for anything short of fire'? Just that, and finished; instead of long earnest discussions[7]. When she heard Harry and Matthew explaining it to the twins with Mrs Parkes coming in[8] – 'Yes, well, a family sometimes gets on top of a woman[9]' – she had to go right away to the bottom of the garden until the devils of exasperation had finished their dance in her blood.

But now there was a room, and she could go there when she liked, she used it seldom[10]: she felt even more caged[11] there than in her bedroom. One day she had gone up there after a

---

1 **coloured chalks:** gizes coloridos • 2 **she was entitled to:** tinha direito a • 3 **not taking Mother for granted:** não menosprezar a mãe • 4 **overheard:** ouviu por acaso • 5 **fuss:** alvoroço • 6 **to fit out:** arrumar • 7 **earnest discussions:** discussões sérias • 8 **with Mrs Parkes coming in:** com a sra. Parkes se intrometendo • 9 **gets on top of a woman:** esgota uma mulher • 10 **seldom:** raramente • 11 **caged:** enjaulada

lunch for ten children she had cooked and served because Mrs Parkes was not there, and had sat alone for a while looking into the garden. She saw the children stream[1] out from the kitchen and stand looking up at the window where she sat behind the curtains. They were all – her children and their friends – discussing Mother's Room. A few minutes later, the chase of children in some game came pounding up the stairs[2], but ended as abruptly as if they had fallen over a ravine[3], so sudden was the silence. They had remembered she was there, and had gone silent in a great gale of 'Hush! Shhhhhh![4] Quiet, you'll disturb her...' And they went tiptoeing[5] downstairs like criminal conspirators. When she came down to make tea for them, they all apologised. The twins put their arms around her, from front and back, making a human cage of loving limbs[6], and promised it would never occur again. 'We forgot. Mummy, we forgot all about it!'

What it amounted to was that Mother's Room, and her need for privacy, had become a valuable lesson in respect for other people's rights. Quite soon Susan was going up to the room only because it was a lesson it was a pity to drop[7]. Then she took sewing up there[8], and the children and Mrs Parkes came in and out: it had become another family room.

She sighed[9], and smiled, and resigned herself[10] – she made jokes at her own expense with Matthew over the room. That is, she did from the self she liked, she respected. But at the same

---

1 **stream:** sair • 2 **the chase of children in some game pounding up the stairs:** o estrépito das crianças brincando de se perseguir nas escadas • 3 **ravine:** barranco • 4 **a great gale of 'Hush! Shhhhhh!':** um grande ruído de shhhhhh! • 5 **tiptoeing:** na ponta dos pés • 6 **a human cage of loving limbs:** uma jaula humana de membros carinhosos • 7 **to drop:** não aproveitar • 8 **she took sewing up there:** ela levou a costura para cima • 9 **she sighed:** ela suspirava • 10 **resigned herself:** se resignava

time, something inside her howled with impatience[1], with rage ... And she was frightened. One day she found herself kneeling by her bed and praying: 'Dear God, keep it away from me, keep him away from me.' She meant the devil, for she now thought of it, not caring if she was irrational, as some sort of demon. She imagined him, or it, as a youngish man, or perhaps a middle-aged man pretending to be young. Or a man young-looking from immaturity? At any rate[2], she saw the young-looking face, which, when she drew closer[3], had dry lines[4] about mouth and eyes. He was thinnish, meagre in build[5]. And he had a reddish complexion, and ginger hair[6]. That was he – a gingery, energetic man, and he wore a reddish hairy jacket, unpleasant to the touch[7].

Well, one day she saw him. She was standing at the bottom of the garden, watching the river ebb[8] past, when she raised her eyes and saw this person, or being, sitting on the white stone bench. He was looking at her, and grinning[9]. In his hand was a long crooked stick[10], which he had picked off the ground, or broken off[11] the tree above him. He was absent-mindedly, out of an absent-minded or freakish impulse of spite[12], using the stick to stir around in the coils of a blindworm or a grass snake[13] (or some kind of snake-like creature: it was whitish and unhealthy to look at[14], unpleasant). The snake was twisting

---

1 **howled with impatience:** urrava com impaciência • 2 **at any rate:** de todo modo • 3 **she drew closer:** se aproximava • 4 **dry lines:** rugas ressecadas • 5 **thinnish, meagre in build:** esbelto, de constituição enxuta • 6 **a reddish complexion, and ginger hair:** uma complexão avermelhada, e cabelo ruivo • 7 **hairy jacket, unpleasant to the touch:** uma jaqueta de pelo desagradável ao toque • 8 **the river ebb:** o fluxo do rio • 9 **grinning:** sorrindo • 10 **crooked stick:** um galho curvo • 11 **broken off:** arrancado • 12 **out of an absent-minded or freakish impulse of spite:** por um impulso descuidado ou caprichoso de maldade • 13 **to stir around in the coils of a blindworm or a grass snake:** para dar voltas nos anéis de uma cobra-de-vidro ou de uma cobra d'água • 14 **whitish and unhealthy to look at:** branquela e desagradável de olhar

about[1], flinging its coils[2] from side to side in a kind of dance of protest against the teasing prodding stick[3].

Susan looked at him, thinking: Who is the stranger? What is he doing in our garden? Then she recognised the man around whom her terrors had crystallised. As she did so, he vanished. She made herself[4] walk over to the bench. A shadow from a branch lay across thin emerald grass[5], moving jerkily[6] over its roughness[7], and she could see why she had taken it for[8] a snake, lashing and twisting[9]. She went back to the house thinking: Right, then, so I've seen him with my own eyes, so I'm not crazy after all – there is a danger because I've seen him. He is lurking[10] in the garden and sometimes even in the house, and he wants *to get into me and to take me over*[11].

She dreamed of having a room or a place, anywhere, where she could go and sit, by herself, no one knowing where she was.

Once, near Victoria, she found herself outside a newsagent[12] that had Rooms to Let[13] advertised. She decided to rent a room, telling no one. Sometimes she could take the train in to Richmond and sit alone in it for an hour or two. Yet how could she? A room would cost three or four pounds a week, and she earned no money, and how could she explain to Matthew that she needed such a sum? What for? It did not occur to her that she was taking it for granted she wasn't going to tell him about the room.

---

1 **twisting about:** se retorcia • 2 **flinging its coils:** sacudindo seus anéis • 3 **the teasing prodding stick:** o galho incômodo que a cutucava • 4 **she made herself:** ela se obrigou • 5 **lay across thin emerald grass:** espalhava sobre a fina grama cor de esmeralda • 6 **moving jerkily:** estremecendo ao mover-se • 7 **roughness:** rusticidade • 8 **she had taken it for:** ela a confundiu com • 9 **lashing and twisting:** que se sacudia e retorcia • 10 **he is lurking:** ele se esconde • 11 **to take me over:** apoderar-se de mim • 12 **newsagent:** banca de jornal • 13 **Rooms to Let:** anúncios de quartos para alugar

Well, it was out of the question, having a room; yet she know she must.

One day, when a school term was well established, and none of the children had measles[1] or other ailments[2], and everything seemed in order, she did the shopping early, explained to Mrs Parkes she was meeting an old school friend, took the train to Victoria, searched until she found a small quiet hotel, and asked for a room for the day. They did not let rooms by the day, the manageress[3] said, looking doubtful[4], since Susan so obviously was not the kind of woman who needed a room for unrespectable reasons. Susan made a long explanation about not being well, being unable to shop without frequent rests[5] for lying down. At last she was allowed to rent the room provided[6] she paid a full night's price for it. She was taken up by the manageress and a maid[7], both concerned over the state of her health... which must be pretty bad if, living at Richmond (she had signed her name and address in the register), she needed a shelter at Victoria.

The room was ordinary and anonymous, and was just what Susan needed. She put a shilling[8] in the gas fire[9], and sat, eyes shut, in a dingy armchair[10] with her back to a dingy window. She was alone. She was alone. She was alone. She could feel pressures lifting off her[11]. First the sounds of traffic came very loud; then they seemed to vanish; she might even have slept a little. A knock on the door: it was Miss Townsend, the manageress, bringing her a cup of tea with her own hands, so concerned was she over Susan's long silence and possible illness.

---

1 **measles:** sarampo • 2 **ailments:** outras doenças • 3 **manageress:** a gerente • 4 **doubtful:** cheia de dúvidas • 5 **rests:** descansos • 6 **provided:** com a condição de • 7 **maid:** faxineira • 8 **shilling:** xelim • 9 **gas fire:** aquecedor a gás • 10 **in a dingy armchair:** uma poltrona suja ou desbotada • 11 **lifting off her:** se afastando dela

Miss Townsend was a lonely woman of fifty, running this hotel with all the rectitude expected of her, and she sensed in Susan the possibility of understanding companionship. She stayed to talk. Susan found herself in the middle of a fantastic story about her illness, which got more and more impossible as she tried to make it tally with the large house at Richmond[1], well-off husband[2], and four children. Suppose she said instead: Miss Townsend, I'm here in your hotel because I need to be alone for a few hours, above all *alone and with no one knowing where I am*. She said it mentally, and saw, mentally, the look that would inevitably come on Miss Townsend's elderly maiden's face[3]. 'Miss Townsend, my four children and my husband are driving me insane, do you understand that? Yes, I can see from the gleam[4] of hysteria in your eyes that comes from loneliness controlled but only just contained[5] that I've got everything in the world you've ever longed for[6]. Well, Miss Townsend, I don't want any of it. You can have it, Miss Townsend. I wish I was absolutely alone in the world, like you. Miss Townsend, I'm besieged[7] by seven devils, Miss Townsend, Miss Townsend, let me stay here in your hotel where the devils can't get me...' Instead of saying all this, she described her anaemia, agreed to try Miss Townsend's remedy for it, which was raw liver, minced, between whole-meal bread[8], and said yes, perhaps it would be better if she stayed at home and let a friend do shopping for her. She paid her bill and left the hotel, defeated[9].

---

1 **as she tried to make it tally with the large house at Richmond:** enquanto ela tentava fazer bater com a grande casa em Richmond • 2 **well-off husband:** o marido bem-sucedido • 3 **elderly maiden's face:** cara de solteirona • 4 **gleam:** brilho • 5 **loneliness controlled but only just contained:** solidão controlada, mas apenas contida • 6 **longed for:** sempre desejou • 7 **besieged:** sitiada • 8 **raw liver, minced, between whole-meal bread:** fígado cru picado no pão integral • 9 **defeated:** derrotada

At home Mrs Parkes said she didn't really like it, no, not really, when Mrs Rawlings was away from nine in the morning until five. The teacher had telephoned from school to say Joan's teeth were paining her, and she hadn't known what to say; and what was she to make for the children's tea, Mrs Rawlings hadn't said.

All this was nonsense, of course. Mrs Parkes's complaint was that Susan had withdrawn herself spiritually, leaving the burden of the big house on her.

Susan looked back at her day of 'freedom' which had resulted in her becoming a friend of the lonely Miss Townsend, and in Mrs Parkes's remonstrances. Yet she remembered the short blissful hour of being alone, really alone. She was determined to arrange her life, no matter what it cost, so that she could have that solitude more often. An absolute solitude, where no one knew her or cared about her.

But how? She thought of saying to her old employer: I want you to back me up[1] in a story with Matthew that I am doing part-time work for you. The truth is that . . . But she would have to tell him a lie too, and which lie? She could not say: I want to sit by myself three or four times a week in a rented room. And besides, he knew Matthew, and she could not really ask him to tell lies on her behalf[2], apart from being bound to think it meant a lover[3].

Suppose she really took a part-time job, which she could get through fast and efficiently, leaving time for herself. What job? Addressing envelopes[4]? Canvassing[5]?

---

1 **I want you to back me up:** quero que você me acoberte • 2 **on her behalf**: em favor dela • 3 **apart from being bound to think it meant a lover:** além de certamente estar propenso a pensar que se tratava de um amante • 4 **addressing envelopes:** endereçar envelopes • 5 **canvassing:** prospectar clientes (como representante comercial)

And there was Mrs Parkes, working widow, who knew exactly what she was prepared to give to the house, who knew by instinct when her mistress[1] withdrew in spirit[2] from her responsibilities. Mrs Parkes was one of the servers of this world, but she needed someone to serve. She had to have Mrs Rawlings, her madam, at the top of the house or in the garden, so that she could come and get support from her: 'Yes, the bread's not what it was when I was a girl . . . Yes, Harry's got a wonderful appetite, I wonder where he puts it all . . . Yes, it's lucky the twins are so much of a size[3], they can wear each other's shoes, that's a saving[4] in these hard times . . . Yes, the cherry jam[5] from Switzerland is not a patch on[6] the jam from Poland, and three times the price . . . ' And so on. That sort of talk Mrs Parkes must have, every day, or she would leave, not knowing herself why she left.

Susan Rawlings, thinking these thoughts, found that she was prowling through the great thicketed garden[7] like a wild cat: she was walking up the stairs, down the stairs, through the rooms into the garden, along the brown running river, back, up through the house, down again . . . It was a wonder[8] Mrs Parkes did not think it strange. But, on the contrary, Mrs Rawlings could do what she liked, she could stand on her head if she wanted, provided she was *there*. Susan Rawlings prowled and muttered[9] through her house, hating Mrs Parkes, hating poor Miss Townsend, dreaming other hour of solitude in the dingy respectability of Miss Townsend's hotel bedroom, and she knew quite well she was mad. Yes, she was mad.

1 **mistress:** patroa • 2 **withdrew in spirit:** se afastava em espírito • 3 **so much of a size:** do mesmo tamanho • 4 **saving:** economia • 5 **cherry jam:** geleia de cereja • 6 **is not a patch on:** não tem comparação • 7 **she was prowling through the great thicketed garden:** estava rondando pelo grande jardim cheio de mato • 8 **it was a wonder:** era incrível • 9 **muttered:** resmungou

She said to Matthew that she must have a holiday. Matthew agreed with her. This was not as things had been once – how they had talked in each other's arms in the marriage bed. He had, she knew, diagnosed her finally as *unreasonable*[1]. She had become someone outside himself that he had to manage. They were living side by side in this house like two tolerably friendly strangers.

Having told Mrs Parkes – or rather, asked for her permission – she went off on a walking holiday[2] in Wales. She chose the remotest place she knew of. Every morning the children telephoned her before they went onto school, to encourage and support her, just as they had over Mother's Room. Every evening she telephoned them, spoke to each child in turn, and then to Matthew. Mrs Parkes, given permission to telephone for instructions or advice, did so every day at lunchtime. When, as happened three times, Mrs Rawlings was out on the mountain-side[3], Mrs Parkes asked that she should ring back at such-and-such a time, for she would not be happy in what she was doing without Mrs Rawlings' blessing[4].

Susan prowled over wild country with the telephone wire[5] holding her to her duty like a leash[6]. The next time she must telephone, or wait to be telephoned, nailed her to her cross[7]. The mountains themselves seemed trammelled[8] by her unfreedom. Everywhere on the mountains, where she met no one at all, from breakfast time to dusk[9], excepting sheep, or a shepherd[10], she came face to face with her own craziness, which

---

1 **unreasonable:** insensata • 2 **she went off on a walking holiday:** ela saiu de férias para fazer caminhadas • 3 **mountain-side:** nas encostas • 4 **without Mrs Rawlings' blessing:** sem a bênção da sra. Rawlings • 5 **telephone wire:** fio de telefone • 6 **holding her to her duty like a leash:** amarrando-a a seu dever como uma coleira • 7 **nailed her to her cross:** a pregava em sua cruz • 8 **trammelled:** presas • 9 **dusk:** entardecer • 10 **shepherd:** pastor

might attack her in the broadest valleys, so that they seemed too small, or on a mountain top from which she could see a hundred other mountains and valleys, so that they seemed too low, too small, with the sky pressing down too close. She would stand gazing at a hillside[1] brilliant with ferns and bracken[2], jewelled with running water[3], and see nothing but her devil, who lifted inhuman eyes at her[4] from where he leaned negligently[5] on a rock, switching[6] at his ugly yellow boots with a leafy twig[7].

She returned to her home and family, with the Welsh emptiness at the back of her mind like a promise of freedom.

She told her husband she wanted to have an *au pair* girl.

They were in their bedroom, it was late at night, the children slept. He sat, shirted and slippered[8], in a chair by the window, looking out. She sat brushing her hair and watching him in the mirror. A time-hallowed scene[9] in the connubial bedroom[10]. He said nothing, while she heard the arguments coming into his mind, only to be rejected[11] because every one was *reasonable*.

'It seems strange to get one now; after all, the children are in school most of the day. Surely the time for you to have help was when you were stuck with them day and night[12]. Why don't you ask Mrs Parkes to cook for you? She's even offered to – I can understand if you are tired of cooking for six people. But

---

1 **hillside**: encosta • 2 **ferns and bracken:** duas espécies diferentes de samambaias • 3 **jewelled with running water:** adornada com água corrente • 4 **who lifted inhuman eyes at her:** que levantou seu olhar inumano sobre ela • 5 **he leaned negligently:** se apoiava desleixadamente • 6 **switching:** batendo • 7 **leafy twig:** um galho com folhas • 8 **shirted and slippered:** de camisa e chinelos • 9 **a time-hallowed scene:** uma cena consagrada no tempo • 10 **connubial bedroom:** dormitório matrimonial • 11 **rejected:** rejeitados • 12 **stuck with them day and night:** presa a eles dia e noite

you know that an *au pair* girl means all kinds of problems; it's not like having an ordinary char[1] in[2] during the day…'

Finally he said carefully: 'Are you thinking of going back to work?'

'No,' she said, 'no, not really.' She made herself sound vague, rather stupid. She went on brushing her black hair and peering at herself so as to be oblivious[3] of the short uneasy glances[4] her Matthew kept giving her. 'Do you think we can't afford it?' she went on vaguely, not at all the old efficient Susan who know exactly what they could afford.

'It's not that,' he said, looking out of the window at dark trees, so as not to look at her. Meanwhile she examined a round, candid, pleasant face with clear dark brows[5] and clear grey eyes[6]. A sensible face. She brushed thick healthy black hair and thought: Yet that's the reflection of a madwoman. How very strange! Much more to the point[7] if what looked back at me was the gingery green-eyed demon with his dry meagre smile[8]… Why wasn't Matthew agreeing? After all, what else could he do? She was breaking her part of the bargain[9] and there was no way of forcing her to keep it[10]: that her spirit, her soul, should live in this house, so that the people in it could grow like plants in water, and Mrs Parkes remain content in their service[11]. In return for this, he would be a good loving husband, and responsible towards the children. Well, nothing like this had been true of either of them for a long time. He did

---

1 **char:** diarista • 2 **in:** em casa • 3 **peering at herself so as to be oblivious:** ela continuava se olhando como se não reparasse • 4 **uneasy glances:** olhares inquietos • 5 **clear dark brows:** com sobrancelhas escuras bem definidas • 6 **clear grey eyes:** olhos cinza-claro • 7 **much more to the point:** seria mais lógico • 8 **dry meagre smile:** sorriso mordaz e mesquinho • 9 **bargain:** trato • 10 **to keep it:** mantê-lo • 11 **remain content in their service:** permanecer satisfeita com seu serviço

his duty, perfunctorily[1]; she did not even pretend[2] to do hers. And he had become like other husbands, with his real life in his work and the people he met there, and very likely[3] a serious affair. All this was her fault.

At last he drew heavy curtains[4], blotting out the trees[5], and turned to force her attention[6]: 'Susan, are you really sure we need a girl?' But she would not meet his appeal[7] at all. She was running the brush over her hair again and again, lifting fine black clouds in a small hiss[8] of electricity. She was peering in[9] and smiling as if she were amused at the clinging hissing hair[10] that followed the brush.

'Yes, I think it would be a good idea, on the whole[11],' she said, with the cunning[12] of a madwoman evading the real point.

In the mirror she could see her Matthew lying on his back, his hands behind his head, staring upwards, his face sad and hard. She felt her heart (the old heart of Susan Rawlings) soften[13] and call out to him[14]. But she set it to be indifferent[15].

He said: 'Susan, the children?' It was an appeal[16] that *almost* reached her. He opened his arms, lifting them palms up[17], empty. She had only to run across and fling herself into them[18], on to his hard, warm chest, and melt into herself, into Susan. But she could not. She would not see his lifted arms. She said

---

1 **perfunctorily:** por mera formalidade; mecanicamente • 2 **she did not even pretend:** ela nem ao menos fingia • 3 **very likely:** muito provavelmente • 4 **he drew heavy curtains:** fechou as cortinas pesadas • 5 **blotting out the trees:** ocultando as árvores • 6 **and turned to force her attention:** e se virou para atrair a atenção dela • 7 **she would not meet his appeal:** mas ela não respondeu ao seu chamado • 8 **a small hiss:** um pequeno chiado • 9 **she was peering in:** tinha o olhar fixo • 10 **the clinging hissing hair:** o chiado persistente do cabelo • 11 **on the whole:** de modo geral • 12 **cunning:** astúcia • 13 **soften:** abrandar-se • 14 **call out to him:** chamar por ele • 15 **she set it to be indifferent:** ela se policiou para manter-se indiferente • 16 **appeal:** súplica • 17 **lifting them palms up:** levantando-os com as palmas para cima • 18 **fling herself into them:** se jogar em seus braços

vaguely[1]: 'Well, surely it'll be even better for them? We'll get a French or a German girl and they'll learn the language.'

In the dark she lay beside him, feeling frozen[2], a stranger. She felt as if Susan had been spirited away[3]. She disliked very much this woman who lay here, cold and indifferent beside a suffering man, but she could not change her.

Next morning she set about getting a girl[4], and very soon came Sophie Traub from Hamburg, a girl of twenty, laughing, healthy, blue-eyed, intending to learn English. Indeed[5], she already spoke a good deal[6]. In return for a room – 'Mother's Room' – and her food, she undertook to do some light cooking[7], and to be with the children when Mrs Rawlings asked. She was an intelligent girl and understood perfectly what was needed. Susan said: 'I go off sometimes, for the morning or for the day – well, sometimes the children run home from school[8], or they ring up[9], or a teacher rings up. I should be here, really. And there's the daily woman[10] . . . ' And Sophie laughed her deep fruity *Fräulein's* laugh[11], showed her fine white teeth and her dimples[12], and said: 'You want some person to play mistress of the house[13] sometimes, not so[14]?'

'Yes, that is just so,' said Susan, a bit dry, despite herself, thinking in secret fear how easy it was, how much nearer to the end she was than she thought. Healthy Fraülein Traub's instant understanding of their position proved this to be true.

---

1 **vaguely:** distraidamente • 2 **feeling frozen:** sentindo gélida • 3 **spirited away:** desaparecido feito fumaça • 4 **she set about getting a girl:** se ocupou em conseguir uma menina • 5 **indeed:** de fato • 6 **a good deal:** bastante • 7 **she undertook to do some light cooking:** se comprometeu a cozinhar um pouco • 8 **run home from school:** voltam da escola para casa • 9 **they ring up:** telefonam • 10 **daily woman:** empregada doméstica • 11 **deep fruity Fräulein's laugh:** gargalhada profunda e sonora de Fräulein ("senhorita", em alemão) • 12 **dimples:** covinhas • 13 **to play mistress of the house:** fazer o papel da dona de casa • 14 **not so?:** não é isso?

The *au pair* girl, because of her own commonsense¹, or (as Susan said to herself, with her new inward shudder²) because she had been *chosen* so well by Susan, was a success with everyone, the children liking her, Mrs Parkes forgetting almost at once that she was German, and Matthew finding her 'nice to have around the house'. For he was now taking things as they came, from the surface of life, withdrawn³ both as a husband and a father from the household⁴.

One day Susan saw how Sophie and Mrs Parkes were talking and laughing in the kitchen, and she announced that she would be away until tea time. She knew exactly where to go and what she must look for. She took the District Line to South Kensington, changed to the Circle, got off at Paddington, and walked around looking at the smaller hotels until she was satisfied with one which had FRED'S HOTEL painted on windowpanes⁵ that needed cleaning. The façade⁶ was a faded shiny yellow⁷, like unhealthy skin. A door at the end of a passage said she must knock; she did, and Fred appeared. He was not at all attractive, not in any way, being fattish, and run-down⁸, and wearing a tasteless striped suit⁹. He had small sharp eyes¹⁰ in a white creased face¹¹, and was quite prepared to let Mrs Jones (she chose the farcical name¹² deliberately, staring him out¹³) have a room three days a week from ten until six. Provided of course that she paid in advance each time she came? Susan produced¹⁴ fifteen shillings (no price had been set by him) and

---

1 **commonsense:** bom senso • 2 **inward shudder:** estremecimento interno • 3 **withdrawn:** tinha se retirado • 4 **household:** lar • 5 **windowpanes:** os vidros da janela • 6 **façade:** fachada • 7 **a faded shiny yellow:** amarelo intenso apagado • 8 **run-down:** desleixado • 9 **a tasteless stripped suit:** um terno listrado de mau gosto • 10 **sharp eyes:** olhos penetrantes • 11 **a white creased face:** um rosto pálido e enrugado • 12 **farcical name:** nome rídiculo • 13 **staring him out:** o encarando • 14 **produced:** pegou

held it out[1], still fixing him with a bold unblinking challenge[2] she had not known until then she could use at will[3]. Looking at her still, he took up a ten-shilling note from her palm between thumb and forefinger[4], fingered it[5]; then shuffled up two half-crowns[6], held out his own palm with these bits of money displayed thereon[7], and let his gaze lower broodingly at them[8]. They were standing in the passage, a red-shaded light above[9], bare boards beneath[10], and a strong smell of floor polish rising about them. He shot his gaze up at her over the still-extended palm, and smiled as if to say: What do you take me for[11]? 'I shan't,' said Susan, 'be using this room for the purposes of making money.' He still waited. She added another five shillings, at which he nodded and said: 'You pay, and I ask no questions.' 'Good,' said Susan. He now went past her to the stairs, and there waited a moment: the light from the street door being in her eyes, she lost sight of him[12] momentarily. Then she saw a sober-suited[13], white-faced, white-balding[14] little man trotting up the stairs[15] like a waiter, and she went after him. They proceeded in utter silence[16] up the stairs of this house where no questions were asked – Fred's Hotel, which could afford the freedom for its visitors that poor Miss Townsend's hotel could not. The room was hideous[17]. It had a single window, with thin green

---

1 **held it out:** lhe entregou • 2 **fixing him with a bold unblinking challenge:** olhando-o fixamente com expressão desafidora e sem pestanejar • 3 **at will:** deliberadamente • 4 **between thumb and forefinger:** entre o polegar e o indicador • 5 **fingered it:** tocou • 6 **shuffled up two half-crowns:** pegou duas moedas de meia coroa • 7 **displayed thereon:** à vista • 8 **let his gaze lower broodingly at them:** deixou que seu olhar caísse sobre elas • 9 **a red-shaded light above:** uma luz avermelhada em cima • 10 **bare boards beneath:** tábuas lisas embaixo • 11 **what do you take me for?:** quem você acha que eu sou? • 12 **she lost sight of him:** ela o perdeu de vista • 13 **sober-suited:** vestido sobriamente • 14 **white-balding:** de careca pálida • 15 **trotting up the stairs:** subindo as escadas rapidamente • 16 **utter silence:** silêncio absoluto • 17 **hideous:** horrível

brocade curtains[1], a three-quarter bed that had a cheap green satin bedspread[2] on it, a fireplace with a gas fire and a shilling meter[3] by it, a chest of drawers[4], and a green wicker armchair[5].

'Thank you,' said Susan, knowing that Fred (if this was Fred, and not George, or Herbert or Charlie) was looking at her, not so much with curiosity, an emotion he would not own to[6], for professional reasons, but with a philosophical sense of what was appropriate. Having taken her money and shown her up and agreed to everything, he was clearly disapproving of her for coming here. She did not belong here at all, so his look said. (But she knew, already, how very much she did belong: the room had been waiting for her to join it.) 'Would you have me called at five o'clock, please?' and he nodded[7] and went downstairs.

It was twelve in the morning. She was free. She sat in the armchair, she simply sat, she closed her eyes and sat and let herself be alone. She was alone and no one knew where she was. When a knock came on the door she was annoyed, and prepared to show it: but it was Fred himself; it was five o'clock and he was calling her as ordered. He flicked his sharp little eyes over the room[8] – bed, first. It was undisturbed. She might never have been in the room at all. She thanked him, said she would be returning the day after tomorrow, and left. She was back home in time to cook supper, to put the children to bed, to cook a second supper for her husband and herself later. And to welcome Sophie back from the pictures[9] where she had gone

---

1 **brocade curtains:** cortinas de brocado • 2 **satin bedspread:** colcha de cetim • 3 **shilling meter:** um aparelho alimentado por moedas • 4 **a chest of drawers:** uma cômoda • 5 **a green wicker armchair:** uma poltrona verde de vime • 6 **he would not own to:** ele não reconheceria • 7 **he nodded:** concordou com a cabeça • 8 **he flicked his sharp little eyes over the room:** olhou para o quarto com seus pequenos olhos penetrantes • 9 **the pictures:** cinema

with a friend. All these things she did cheerfully, willingly¹. But she was thinking all the time of the hotel room; she was longing for it² with her whole being.

Three times a week. She arrived promptly³ at ten, looked Fred in the eyes, gave him twenty shillings, followed him up the stairs, went into the room, and shut the door on him with gentle firmness⁴. For Fred, disapproving of her being here at all, was quite ready to let friendship, or at least acquaintance-ship⁵, follow his disapproval, if only she would let him. But he was content to go off on her dismissing nod⁶, with the twenty shillings in his hand.

She sat in the armchair and shut her eyes.

What did she *do* in the room? Why, nothing at all⁷. From the chair, when it had rested her⁸, she went to the window, stretching her arms, smiling, treasuring her anonymity⁹, to look out¹⁰. She was no longer Susan Rawlings, mother of four, wife of Matthew, employer of Mrs Parkes and of Sophie Traub, with these and those relations with friends, school-teachers, tradesmen¹¹. She no longer was mistress of the big white house and garden, owning clothes suitable¹² for this and that activity or occasion. She was Mrs Jones, and she was alone, and she had no past and no future. Here I am, she thought, after all these years of being married and having children and playing those roles of responsibility – and I'm just the same. Yet there have been times I thought that nothing existed of me except the roles that

---

1 **willingly:** com prazer • 2 **she was longing for it:** ansiando por ele • 3 **promptly:** pontualmente • 4 **gentle firmness:** com amável firmeza • 5 **acquaintanceship:** convivência entre conhecidos • 6 **on her dismissing nod:** no seu gesto de despedida • 7 **why, nothing at all:** ora, absolutamente nada • 8 **when it had rested her:** quando já tinha descansado • 9 **treasuring her anonymity:** valorizando seu anonimato • 10 **look out:** olhar para fora • 11 **tradesmen:** comerciantes • 12 **suitable:** adequadas

went with being Mrs Matthew Rawlings. Yes, here I am, and if I never saw any of my family again, here I would still be... how very strange that is! And she leaned on the sill[1], and looked into the street, loving the men and women who passed, because she did not know them. She looked at the downtrodden[2] buildings over the street, and at the sky, wet and dingy, or sometimes blue, and she felt she had never seen buildings or sky before. And then she went back to the chair, empty, her mind a blank[3]. Sometimes she talked aloud, saying nothing – an exclamation, meaningless, followed by a comment about the floral pattern on the thin rug[4], or a stain on the green satin coverlet[5]. For the most part, she wool-gathered[6] – what word is there for it? – brooded[7], wandered[8], simply went dark[9], feeling emptiness run deliciously through her veins like the movement of her blood.

This room had become more her own than the house she lived in. One morning she found Fred taking her a flight higher[10] than usual. She stopped, refusing to go up, and demanded[11] her usual room, Number 19. 'Well, you'll have to wait half an hour, then,' he said. Willingly she descended to the dark disinfectant-smelling hall, and sat waiting until the two, man and woman, came down the stairs, giving her swift indifferent glances[12] before they hurried out[13] into the street, separating at the door. She went up to the room, *her* room, which they had

---

1 **she leaned on the sill:** ela se inclinou no peitoril • 2 **downtrodden:** apertados • 3 **her mind a blank:** a mente em branco • 4 **the floral pattern on the thin rug:** o padrão floral do tapete desgastado • 5 **a stain on the green satin coverlet:** uma mancha na colcha de cetim verde • 6 **she wool-gathered:** pensava na morte da bezerra • 7 **brooded:** meditava • 8 **wandered:** divagava • 9 **simply went dark:** simplesmente ficava no escuro • 10 **a flight higher:** um andar acima • 11 **demanded:** exigiu • 12 **swift indifferent glances:** rápidos olhares indiferentes • 13 **they hurried out:** saírem apressados

just vacated¹. It was no less hers, though the windows were set wide open, and a maid was straightening² the bed as she came in.

After these days of solitude, it was both easy to play her part³ as mother and wife, and difficult – because it was so easy: she felt an imposter. She felt as if her shell⁴ moved here, with her family, answering to Mummy, Mother, Susan, Mrs Rawlings. She was surprised no one saw through her⁵, that she wasn't turned out of doors⁶, as a fake⁷. On the contrary, it seemed the children loved her more; Matthew and she 'got on' pleasantly⁸, and Mrs Parkes was happy in her work under⁹ (for the most part, it must be confessed) Sophie Traub. At night she lay beside her husband, and they made love again, apparently just as they used to, when they were really married. But she, Susan, or the being who answered so readily and improbably¹⁰ to the name of Susan, was not there: she was in Fred's Hotel, in Paddington, waiting for the easing hours¹¹ of solitude to begin.

Soon she made a new arrangement with Fred and with Sophie. It was for five days a week. As for the money, five pounds, she simply asked Matthew for it. She saw that she was not even frightened he might ask what for: he would give it to her, she know that, and yet it was terrifying it could be so, for this close couple, these partners, had once known the destination of every shilling they must spend. He agreed to give her five pounds a week. She asked for just so much, not a penny more.

---

1 **they had just vacated:** que tinham acabado de liberar • 2 **straightening the bed:** arrumando a cama • 3 **to play her part:** fazer o seu papel • 4 **shell:** concha • 5 **no one saw through her:** ninguém a tinha descoberto • 6 **that she wasn't turned out of doors:** que não era despejada • 7 **as a fake:** como uma impostora • 8 **got on pleasantly:** se davam bastante bem • 9 **under:** sob as ordens de • 10 **so readily and improbably:** tão imediata e surpreendentemente • 11 **the easing hours:** as plácidas horas

He sounded indifferent about it. It was as if he were paying her, she thought: *paying her off*[1] – yes, that was it. Terror came back for a moment when she understood this, but she stilled it[2]: things had gone too far for that. Now, every week, on Sunday nights, he gave her five pounds, turning away from her before their eyes could meet on the transaction. As for Sophie Traub, she was to be somewhere in or near the house until six at night, after which she was free. She was not to cook, or to clean; she was simply to be there. So she gardened or sewed[3], and asked friends in[4], being a person who was bound to[5] have a lot of friends. If the children were sick, she nursed them[6]. If teachers telephoned, she answered them sensibly[7]. For the five daytimes[8] in the school week, she was altogether the mistress of the house.

One night in the bedroom, Matthew asked: 'Susan, I don't want to interfere – don't think that, please – but are you sure you are well?'

She was brushing her hair at the mirror. She made two more strokes[9] on either side of her head, before she replied: 'Yes, dear, I am sure I am well.'

He was again lying on his back, his blonde head on his hands, his elbows angled up and part concealing[10] his face. He said: 'Then Susan, I have to ask you this question, though you must understand, I'm not putting any sort of pressure on you.' (Susan heard the word 'pressure' with dismay[11], because this was inevitable; of course she could not go on like this.) 'Are things going to go on like this?'

---

1 **paying her off:** pagando para se livrar dela • 2 **she stilled it:** o controlou • 3 **she gardened or sewed:** cuidava do jardim ou costurava • 4 **asked friends in:** convidava amigos • 5 **was bound to:** destinada a • 6 **she nursed them:** cuidava deles • 7 **sensibly:** com bom senso, critério • 8 **daytimes:** dias • 9 **strokes:** escovadas • 10 **angled up and part concealing:** levantados, escondendo parcialmente • 11 **dismay:** consternação

'Well,' she said, going vague and bright[1] and idiotic again, so as to escape: 'Well, I don't see why not.'

He was jerking his elbows up and down[2], in annoyance or in pain[3], and, looking at him, she saw he had got thin, even gaunt[4]; and restless angry movements[5] were not what she remembered of him. He said: 'Do you want a divorce, is that it?'

At this, Susan only with the greatest difficulty stopped herself from laughing[6]: she could hear the bright bubbling laughter[7] she *would* have emitted, had she let herself[8]. He could only mean one thing: she had a lover, and that was why she spent her days in London, as lost to him as if she had vanished to another continent.

Then the small panic set in[9] again: she understood that he hoped she did have a lover, he was begging her to say so, because otherwise it would be too terrifying.

She thought this out as she brushed her hair, watching the fine black stuff fly up[10] to make its little clouds of electricity, hiss, hiss, hiss. Behind her head, across the room, was a blue wall. She realised she was absorbed in watching the black hair making shapes against the blue[11]. She should be answering him. 'Do *you* want a divorce, Matthew?'

He said: 'That surely isn't the point, is it?'

'You brought it up[12], I didn't,' she said, brightly, suppressing meaningless tinkling laughter[13].

---

1 **bright:** enérgica • 2 **he was jerking his elbows up and down:** sacudia os cotovelos para cima e para baixo • 3 **in annoyance or in pain:** por irritação ou dor • 4 **gaunt:** descarnado • 5 **restless angry movements:** movimentos raivosos contínuos • 6 **stopped herself from laughing:** conteve seu riso • 7 **bubbling laughter:** gargalhada exagerada • 8 **had she let herself:** se ela tivesse se permitido • 9 **set in:** se instalou • 10 **watching the fine black stuff fly up:** observando os finos fios de cabelo voando • 11 **making shapes against the blue:** desenhando formas contra o fundo azul • 12 **you brought it up:** você que trouxe o assunto à tona (você é quem disse) • 13 **suppressing meaningless tinkling laughter:** contendo um riso sarcástico e sem sentido

Next day she asked Fred: 'Have enquiries been made for me[1]?'

He hesitated, and she said: 'I've been coming here a year now. I've made no trouble, and you've been paid every day. I have a right to be told.'

'As a matter of fact, Mrs Jones, a man did come asking.'

'A man from a detective agency?'

'Well, he could have been, couldn't he?'

'I was asking you . . . Well, what did you tell him?'

'I told him a Mrs Jones came every weekday from ten until five or six and stayed in Number 19 by herself[2].'

'Describing me?'

'Well, Mrs Jones, I had no alternative. Put yourself in my place.'

'By rights I should deduct[3] what that man gave you for the information.'

He raised shocked eyes[4]: she was not the sort of person to make jokes like this! Then he chose to laugh: a pinkish wet slit[5] appeared across; his white crinkled[6] face; his eyes positively[7] begged her to laugh, otherwise he might lose some money. She remained grave[8], looking at him.

He stopped laughing and said: 'You want to go up now?' – returning to the familiarity, the comradeship[9], of the country where no questions are asked, on which (and he knew it) she depended completely.

She went up to sit in her wicker chair. But it was not the same. Her husband had searched her out[10]. (The world had

---

1 **have enquiries been made for me?**: alguém perguntou por mim? • 2 **by herself**: sozinha • 3 **by rights I should deduct:** por direito deveria descontar • 4 **shocked eyes:** olhar surpreso • 5 **pinkish wet slit:** uma fenda rosada e úmida • 6 **crinkled:** enrrugada • 7 **positively:** decididamente • 8 **grave:** séria • 9 **comradeship:** camaradagem • 10 **had searched her out:** a tinha procurado

searched her out.) The pressures were on her. She was here with his connivance[1]. He might walk in at any moment, here, into Room 19. She imagined the report from the detective agency: 'A woman calling herself Mrs Jones, fitting[2] the description of your wife (et cetera, et cetera, et cetera), stays alone all day in Room No. 19. She insists on this room, waits for it if it is engaged[3]. As far as the proprietor knows, she receives no visitors there, male or female.' A report something on these lines[4] Matthew must have received.

Well, of course he was right: things couldn't go on like this. He had put an end to it all simply by sending the detective after her.

She tried to shrink herself back into the shelter of the room[5], a snail pecked out of its shell and trying to squirm back[6]. But the peace of the room had gone. She was trying consciously to revive it, trying to let go into the dark creative trance (or whatever it was) that she had found there. It was no use, yet she craved for it[7], she was as ill as a suddenly deprived addict[8].

Several times she returned to the room, to look for herself there, but instead she found the unnamed spirit of restlessness[9], a pricking fevered hunger[10] for movement, an irritable self-consciousness that made her brain feel as if it had coloured lights going on and off[11] inside it. Instead of the soft dark that had been the room's air, were now waiting for her demons that

---

1 **connivance:** conivência • 2 **fitting:** que se encaixa • 3 **engaged:** ocupado • 4 **something on these lines:** alguma coisa nesse sentido • 5 **tried to shrink herself back into the shelter of the room:** ela tentou se refugiar novamente no abrigo do quarto • 6 **a snail pecked out of its shell and trying to squirm back:** um caracol arrancado de sua concha que tenta entrar de novo, se retorcendo • 7 **she craved for it:** ansiava por isso • 8 **a suddenly deprived addict:** como um viciado forçado à abstinência • 9 **the unnamed spirit of restlesness:** o espírito anônimo da inquietude • 10 **a pricking fevered hunger:** uma pontada de ânsia febril • 11 **going on and off:** acendendo e apagando

made her dash blindly about[1], muttering words of hate; she was impelling herself[2] from point to point like a moth dashing itself against a windowpane[3], sliding[4] to the bottom, fluttering off[5] on broken wings, then crashing into the invisible barrier again. And again and again. Soon she was exhausted, and she told Fred that for a while she would not be needing the room, she was going on holiday. Home she went, to the big white house by the river. The middle of a weekday, and she felt guilty at returning to her own home when not expected. She stood unseen[6], looking in at the kitchen window. Mrs Parkes, wearing a discarded floral overall of Susan's[7], was stooping[8] to slide something into the oven. Sophie, arms folded[9], was leaning her back against a cupboard and laughing at some joke made by a girl not seen before by Susan – a dark foreign girl, Sophie's visitor. In an armchair Molly, one of the twins, lay curled[10], sucking her thumb[11] and watching the grown-ups[12]. She must have some sickness, to be kept from school[13]. The child's listless[14] face, the dark circles under her eyes, hurt Susan: Molly was looking at the three grown-ups working and talking in exactly the same way Susan looked at the four through the kitchen window: she was remote, shut off from them[15].

But then, just as Susan imagined herself going in, picking up the little girl, and sitting in an armchair with her, stroking[16] her

---

1 **dash blindly about:** mover-se num ímpeto cego • 2 **she was impelling herself:** ela se impelia • 3 **like a moth dashing itself against a windowpane:** como uma mariposa que se joga contra o vidro de uma janela • 4 **sliding:** deslizando • 5 **fluttering off:** batendo as asas • 6 **she stood unseen:** ela permaneceu escondida • 7 **a discarded floral overall of Susan's:** um velho macacão florido de Susan • 8 **was stooping:** se inclinava • 9 **arms folded:** de braços cruzados • 10 **lay curled:** estava encolhida • 11 **sucking her thumb:** chupando o dedo • 12 **grown-ups:** adultos • 13 **to be kept from school:** não ter ido à escola • 14 **listless:** apática • 15 **shut off from them:** isolada deles • 16 **stroking:** acariciando

probably heated forehead[1], Sophie did just that: she had been standing on one leg, the other knee flexed, its foot set against the wall. Now she let her foot in its ribbon-tied red shoe[2] slide down the wall, stood solid on two feet, clapping her hands[3] before and behind her, and sang a couple of lines in German, so that the child lifted her heavy eyes at her and began to smile. Then she walked, or rather skipped[4], over to the child, swung her up[5], and let her fall into her lap[6] at the same moment she sat herself. She said 'Hopla! Hopla! Molly . . .' and began stroking the dark untidy young head that Molly laid on her shoulder for comfort.

Well . . . Susan blinked the tears of farewell out of her eyes[7], and went quietly up through the house to her bedroom. There she sat looking at the river through the trees. She felt at peace, but in a way that was new to her. She had no desire to move, to talk, to do anything at all. The devils that had haunted the house, the garden, were not there; but she knew it was because her soul was in Room 19 in Fred's Hotel; she was not really here at all. It was a sensation that should have been frightening: to sit at her own bedroom window, listening to Sophie's rich young voice sing German nursery songs[8] to her child, listening to Mrs Parkes clatter[9] and move below, and to know that all this had nothing to do with her: she was already out of it.

Later, she made herself go down and say she was home: it was unfair to be here unannounced. She took lunch with Mrs Parkes, Sophie, Sophie's Italian friend Maria, and her daughter Molly, and felt like a visitor.

---

1 **heated forehead:** sua testa febril • 2 **ribbon-tied red shoe:** sapato vermelho de cadarços • 3 **clapping her hands:** batendo palmas • 4 **skipped:** pulou • 5 **swung her up:** jogou-a para cima • 6 **lap:** colo • 7 **blinked the tears of farewell out of her eyes:** piscou para afastar as lágrimas de despedida dos olhos • 8 **nursery songs:** canções de ninar • 9 **clatter:** tagarelar

A few days later, at bedtime, Matthew said: 'Here's your five pounds,' and pushed them over at her. Yet he must have known she had not been leaving the house at all.

She shook her head[1], gave it back to him, and said, in explanation, not in accusation: 'As soon as you knew where I was, there was no point.'

He nodded, not looking at her. He was turned away from her[2]: thinking, she knew, how best to handle[3] this wife who terrified him.

He said: 'I wasn't trying to... It's just that I was worried.'

'Yes, I know.'

'I must confess that I was beginning to wonder . . .'

'You thought I had a lover?'

'Yes, I am afraid I did.'

She knew that he wished she had. She sat wondering how to say: 'For a year now I've been spending all my days in a very sordid hotel room. It's the place where I'm happy. In fact, without it I don't exist.' She heard herself saying this, and understood how terrified he was that she might. So instead she said: 'Well, perhaps you're not far wrong.'

Probably Matthew would think the hotel proprietor lied: he would want to think so.

'Well,' he said, and she could hear his voice spring up[4], so to speak, with relief[5], 'in that case I must confess I've got a bit of an affair on myself.'

She said, detached[6] and interested: 'Really? Who is she?' and saw Matthew's startled look[7] because of this reaction.

'It's Phil. Phil Hunt.'

She had known Phil Hunt well in the old unmarried days.

---

1 **she shook her head:** ela balançou a cabeça • 2 **turned away from her:** ficou de costas pra ela • 3 **to handle:** lidar • 4 **spring up:** levantar • 5 **relief:** alívio • 6 **detached:** desapegada • 7 **startled look:** olhar espantado

She was thinking: No, she won't do, she's too neurotic and difficult. She's never been happy yet. Sophie's much better. Well, Matthew will see that himself, as sensible as he is.

This line of thought went on in silence, while she said aloud[1]: 'It's no point telling you about mine, because you don't know him.'

Quick, quick, invent, she thought. Remember how you invented all that nonsense for Miss Townsend.

She began slowly, careful not to contradict herself: 'His name is Michael' *(Michael What?)* – 'Michael Plant.' (What a silly name!) 'He's rather like you – in looks[2], I mean.' And indeed, she could imagine herself being touched by no one but Matthew himself. 'He's a publisher.' (Really? Why?) 'He's got a wife already and two children.'

She brought out[3] this fantasy, proud of herself.

Matthew said: 'Are you two thinking of marrying?'

She said, before she could stop herself: 'Good God[4], *no*!'

She realised, if Matthew wanted to marry Phil Hunt, that this was too emphatic, but apparently[5] it was all right, for his voice sounded relieved as he said: 'It is a bit impossible to imagine oneself married to anyone else, isn't it?' With which he pulled her to him[6], so that her head lay on his shoulder. She turned her face into the dark of his flesh[7], and listened to the blood pounding[8] through her ears saying: I am alone, I am alone, I am alone.

In the morning Susan lay in bed while he dressed.

He had been thinking things out in the night, because now he said: 'Susan, why don't we make a foursome[9]?'

---

1 **aloud:** em voz alta • 2 **in looks:** na aparência • 3 **she brought out:** ela inventou • 4 **Good God:** Meu bom Deus • 5 **apparently:** pelo visto • 6 **with which he pulled her to him:** puxou-a para perto dele • 7 **flesh:** carne • 8 **pounding:** batendo • 9 **foursome:** quarteto

Of course, she said to herself, of course he would be bound to say that[1]. If one is sensible, if one is reasonable, if one never allows oneself a base thought[2] or an envious emotion[3], naturally one says: Let's make a foursome!

'Why not?' she said.

'We could all meet for lunch. I mean, it's ridiculous, you sneaking off to filthy hotels[4], and me staying late at the office, and all the lies everyone has to tell.'

What on earth did I say his name was? – she panicked, then said: 'I think it's a good idea, but Michael is away at the moment. When he comes back, though – and I'm sure you two would like each other.'

'He's away, is he? So that's why you've been…' Her husband put his hand to the knot[5] of his tie in a gesture of male coquetry[6] she would not before have associated with him; and he bent[7] to kiss her cheek with the expression that goes with the words: Oh you naughty little puss[8]! And she felt its answering look, naughty and coy[9], come on to her face.

Inside she was dissolving in horror at them both, at how far they had both sunk from honesty of emotion[10].

So now she was saddled[11] with a lover, and he had a mistress[12]! How ordinary, how reassuring[13], how jolly[14]! And now they would make a foursome of it, and go about[15] to theatres and restaurants. After all, the Rawlingses could well afford[16] that sort of thing, and presumably the publisher Michael Plant

---

1 **he would be bound to say that:** ele estava destinado a dizer isso • 2 **a base thought:** um pensamento vil • 3 **an envious emotion:** um sentimento de inveja • 4 **sneaking off to filthy hotels** esgueirando para hotéis imundos • 5 **knot:** nó • 6 **coquetry:** vaidade • 7 **he bent:** se curvou • 8 **you naughty little puss!:** gatinha safada! • 9 **coy:** tímida • 10 **they had both sunk from honesty of emotion:** os dois tinham se afastado dos sentimentos sinceros • 11 **she was saddled:** estava presa • 12 **mistress:** amante • 13 **reassuring:** reconfortante • 14 **jolly:** divertido • 15 **go about:** sair • 16 **afford:** permitir-se

could afford to do himself and his mistress quite well[1]. No, there was nothing to stop the four of them developing the most intricate relationship of civilised tolerance, all enveloped[2] in a charming afterglow[3] of autumnal passion. Perhaps they would all go off on holidays together? She had known people who did: Or perhaps Matthew would draw the line[4] there? Why should he, though, if he was capable of talking about 'foursomes' at all?

She lay in the empty bedroom, listening to the car drive off with Matthew in it, off to work. Then she heard the children clattering off[5] to school to the accompaniment of Sophie's cheerfully ringing voice[6]. She slid down[7] into the hollow[8] of the bed, for shelter against her own irrelevance. And she stretched out her hand[9] to the hollow where her husband's body had lain[10], but found no comfort there: he was not her husband. She curled herself up in a small tight ball[11] under the clothes: she could stay here all day, all week, indeed, all her life.

But in a few days she must produce Michael Plant, and – but how? She must presumably find some agreeable man prepared to impersonate[12] a publisher called Michael Plant. And in return for which[13] she would – what? Well, for one thing[14] they would make love. The idea made her want to cry with sheer exhaustion. Oh no, she had finished with all that – the proof of it was that the words 'make love', or even imagining it, trying hard to revive no more than the pleasures of sensuality,

---

1 **could afford to do himself and his mistress quite well:** podia permitir-se uma boa vida para ele e para a sua amante • 2 **enveloped:** envolvidos • 3 **afterglow:** resplendor • 4 **would draw the line:** colocaria um limite • 5 **clattering off:** saindo em algazarra • 6 **cheerfully ringing voice:** voz alegre e definida • 7 **she slid down:** ela deslizou • 8 **hollow:** vazio • 9 **she stretched out her hand:** estendeu a mão • 10 **had lain:** havia deitado • 11 **tight ball:** pequena bola • 12 **to impersonate:** fazer-se passar por • 13 **in return for which:** e em troca disso • 14 **for one thing:** para começar

let alone[1] affection, or love, made her want to run away and hide from the sheer effort of the thing . . . Good Lord, why make love at all? Why make love with anyone? Or if you are going to make love, what does it matter who with? Why shouldn't she simply walk into the street, pick up[2] a man and have a roaring sexual affair[3] with him? Why not? Or even with Fred? What difference did it make?

But she had let herself in for it[4] — an interminable stretch of time with a lover, called Michael, as part of a gallant civilised foursome. Well, she could not, and she would not.

She got up, dressed, went down to find Mrs Parkes, and asked her for the loan[5] of a pound, since Matthew, she said, had forgotten to leave her money. She exchanged with Mrs Parkes variations on the theme that husbands are all the same, they don't think, and without saying a word to Sophie, whose voice could be heard upstairs from the telephone, walked to the underground, travelled to South Kensington, changed to the Inner Circle, got out at Paddington, and walked to Fred's Hotel. There she told Fred that she wasn't going on holiday after all, she needed the room. She would have to wait an hour, Fred said. She went to a busy tearoom-cum-restaurant[6] around the corner, and sat watching the people flow in and out the door[7] that kept swinging open and shut[8], watched them mingle and merge[9], and separate, felt her being flow into them, into their movement. When the hour was up[10], she left a half-crown for her pot of tea, and left the place without looking back at it, just as she had left her house, the big, beautiful white house, without

---

1 **let alone:** ainda menos • 2 **pick up:** escolher • 3 **a roaring sexual affair:** uma aventura sexual selvagem • 4 **she had let herself in for it:** ela se deixou levar por aquela situação • 5 **loan:** empréstimo • 6 **tearoom-cum-restaurant:** salão de chá e restaurante • 7 **flow in and flow out the door:** entrando e saindo pela porta • 8 **kept swinging open and shut:** permanecia abrindo e fechando • 9 **mingle and merge:** misturar-se e fundir-se • 10 **the hour was up:** havia passado a hora

another look, but silently dedicating it to Sophie. She returned to Fred, received the key of Number 19, now free, and ascended the grimy[1] stairs slowly, letting floor after floor fall away below her, keeping her eyes lifted[2], so that floor after floor descended jerkily[3] to her level of vision, and fell away out of sight[4].

Number 19 was the same. She saw everything with an acute, narrow, checking glance[5]: the cheap shine of the satin spread[6], which had been replaced carelessly after the two bodies had finished their convulsions under it; a trace of powder[7] on the glass that topped[8] the chest of drawers; an intense green shade in a fold[9] of the curtain. She stood at the window, looking down, watching people pass and pass and pass until her mind went dark from the constant movement. Then she sat in the wicker chair, letting herself go slack[10]. But she had to be careful, because she did not want, today, to be surprised by Fred's knock at five o'clock.

The demons were not here. They had gone for ever, because she was buying her freedom from them. She was slipping already into the dark fructifying dream that seemed to caress her inwardly[11], like the movement of her blood . . . but she had to think about Matthew first. Should she write a letter for the coroner[12]? But what should she say? She would like to leave him with the look on his face she had seen this morning – banal, admittedly[13], but at least confidently healthy[14]. Well, that was impossible, one did not look like that with a wife dead from suicide. But how to leave him believing she was dying

---

1 **grimy:** imundas • 2 **keeping her eyes lifted:** mantendo seus olhos levantados • 3 **jerkily:** vertiginosamente • 4 **fell away out of sight:** desaparecendo da sua vista • 5 **an acute, narrow, checking glance:** um olhar rápido, preciso e profundo • 6 **spread:** colcha • 7 **a trace of powder:** um rastro de pó • 8 **topped:** que ficava em cima • 9 **fold:** dobra • 10 **go slack:** relaxar • 11 **to caress her inwardly:** acariciá-la por dentro • 12 **coroner:** juiz investigador • 13 **admittedly:** tem que admitir • 14 **confidently healthy:** sem dúvida saudável

because of a man – because of the fascinating publisher Michael Plant? Oh, how ridiculous! How absurd! How humiliating! But she decided not to trouble about it, simply not to think about the living[1]. If he wanted to believe she had a lover, he would believe it. And he *did* want to believe it. Even when he had found out that there was no publisher in London called Michael Plant, he would think: Oh poor Susan, she was afraid to give me his real name.

And what did it matter whether he married Phil Hunt or Sophie? Though it ought to be Sophie, who was already the mother of those children . . . and what hypocrisy to sit here worrying about the children, when she was going to leave them because she had not got the energy to stay.

She had about four hours. She spent them delightfully, darkly, sweetly, letting herself slide gently[2], gently, to the edge[3] of the river. Then, with hardly[4] a break in her consciousness, she got up, pushed the thin rug against the door, made sure the windows were tight shut[5], put two shillings in the meter, and turned on the gas. For the first time since she had been in the room she lay on the hard bed that smelled stale[6], that smelled of sweat[7] and sex.

She lay on her back on the green satin cover, but her legs were chilly[8]. She got up, found a blanket folded[9] in the bottom of the chest of drawers, and carefully covered her legs with it. She was quite content lying there, listening to the faint[10] soft hiss of the gas that poured into the room[11], into her lungs, into her brain, as she drifted off into the dark river[12].

---

1 **the living:** os vivos • 2 **gently:** suavemente • 3 **the edge:** a beira • 4 **hardly:** apenas • 5 **tight shut:** bem fechadas • 6 **smelled stale:** cheirava a ranço • 7 **sweat:** suor • 8 **chilly:** frias • 9 **a blanket folded:** um cobertor dobrado • 10 **faint:** fraco • 11 **poured into the room:** que inundava o quarto • 12 **she drifted off into the dark river:** se deixou levar, à deriva, no rio escuro

1ª edição fevereiro de 2011 | **Diagramação** Patrícia De Michelis
Fonte Bembo e Berthold Akzidenz Grotesk | **Papel** Chamois 75g/m²
Impressão e acabamento Yangraf